THE FLAUNTING MOON

Purity Makin is only a girl when James Rodale, a handsome cavalier, seeks shelter at Ladymoon Manor, the house on the moors which holds strange echoes of its sinister past. But the girl has the passions of a woman, and from the events of a night springs a tale of promises betrayed and twisted jealousies; a tale in which a sacred chalice is used for good or evil to satisfy the desires of those who discover the secret of the Moon Goddess.

Books by Catherine Darby
in the Linford Romance Library:

FROST ON THE MOON

CATHERINE DARBY

THE FLAUNTING MOON

Complete and Unabridged

LINFORD
Leicester

First published in Great Britain in 1979 by
Robert Hale Limited
London

First Linford Edition
published 1999
by arrangement with
Robert Hale Limited
London

Copyright © 1979 by Catherine Darby
All rights reserved

British Library CIP Data

Darby, Catherine, *1935* –
The flaunting moon.—Large print ed.—
Linford romance library
1. Love stories
2. Large type books
I. Title
823.9'14 [F]

ISBN 0–7089–5437–5

Published by
F. A. Thorpe (Publishing) Ltd.
Anstey, Leicestershire

Set by Words & Graphics Ltd.
Anstey, Leicestershire
Printed and bound in Great Britain by
T. J. International Ltd., Padstow, Cornwall

This book is printed on acid-free paper

Part One

1644

1

When Purity was small and had been punished she slipped away from the rest of the family and, staring at her pointed face in the glass on her bedside table, repeated over and over, 'I am not the real child of my parents. They found me in a basket on the doorstep. I am not the real child of my parents. They found me — '

Over and over she would repeat the words until the smarting of her buttocks had dulled to an ache and her eyes were only slightly red-rimmed with the tears she was too proud to shed in front of her father.

As she grew into young womanhood it became easier to imagine that she was not really Purity Makin, but a changeling brought up out of charity at Ladymoon Manor, for in appearance and temperament she was completely different from her two brothers and two sisters. Elisha and Luther were grave, brown-haired copies of their father, Sir Joshua. Hope and Mercy had fair hair and delicate complexions resembling the miniature portrait of their mother, who had died when her fifth child was born. Purity had hair so dark that it was almost black and eyes that were brown as the streaks on pansy petals. Her skin had a faint honey tinge and her mouth tilted up at one corner, so that even when she was at her most respectful, she always looked as if she were secretly mocking.

'A God-fearing maid ought to cast down her eyes and curb ungodly mirth,' her father said time and time again.

Obediently Purity would lower her eyes and tuck in her lips primly, but her long lashes made shadows on her cheek-bones and the little pulse in her slender neck throbbed with suppressed laughter.

'You have the manners of a kitchen wench,' her father would say. 'Go to your room, child, and pray the Lord to guide your feet into the paths of righteousness!'

Purity shared a bedroom with Mercy, while Hope, being the eldest daughter, had a slightly smaller apartment next to her. Her two brothers had separate rooms opening off an upper corridor, while her father appropriated to himself the large bedroom at the other side of the house. A lower passage separated this room from where the girls slept. Another short passage and a flight of steps led to the two small rooms where Aunt Hepzibah spent most of her time.

Ladymoon Manor was full of such corridors and unexpected steps leading to airy, low-ceilinged rooms. There was even a secret staircase concealed in the thickness of the wall behind the fireplace. The parlour and the kitchen were part of the original house built with stones taken from an abandoned convent that had once stood by the river. A side hall and a large parlour had been added later in the reign of Queen Bess.

The manor stood solidly high on the moor above the river about half a day's ride from York. All around were the slopes, heather-clad in summer, snow-blanketed in winter, wandering sheep and wild ponies grazed the short, sweet grass and eagles swooped low, hovering on the wind as the lambs scampered below unaware of danger.

Purity had never been to York though sometimes, on a clear day, she fancied she could see the grey walls of the city rising sheer against the blue sky. Her grandparents had lived in York but they, like her mother, were long since dead, and Purity had never seen the house where they had lived or the churchyard where they were buried. She pictured the city as a place of glittering excitement with beautiful houses and gardens gay with flowers, but her father declared it was a cesspool of vice and debauchery, and went there as seldom as possible, except on the most urgent business.

It was more than a year now since either Sir Joshua or his two sons had ridden to York, for the city was held by the Royalists. The war between King and Parliament had begun when Purity was eleven and two years later still raged furiously up and down the country. The Makins supported the Parliament and offered up daily prayers for the gallant soldiers who fought against the tyrannical King and his French Queen.

'Henrietta Maria holds Mass openly in her chapel!' Sir Joshua had thundered. 'She would fill this land of ours with Spanish priests and French nuns. The King listens to her more than he ever listened to his ministers and he places the affairs of his army in the hands of his vile nephew, Prince Rupert.'

Prince Rupert, in the eyes of Sir Joshua, was even more reprehensible than the Pope, for the Pope, being a Catholic, might be excused on the grounds of ignorance but Prince Rupert had been reared as a Lutheran.

'And now secretly worships the Devil, holding rituals in the honour of hell, taking everywhere with him his familiar spirit in the form of a white dog.'

'If he worships the devil in secret,' Purity enquired with interest, 'how comes it to be known?'

'God reveals such things to his servants,' Sir Joshua said.

'And does God reveal the truth about familiar spirits too?' Purity asked.

'God reveals all things needful for salvation,' her father said.

Purity wondered what salvation had to do with white dogs and princes who held strange rituals, but Aunt Hepzibah had caught her eye and was shaking her head.

Aunt Hepzibah was Sir Joshua's younger sister, though Purity doubted if she had ever truly been a girl. Hepzibah Makin was a frail, mousy woman who crept about as if she were in mortal terror of the world and never raised her voice about a whisper. She had a kind heart, however, and in the past when Sir Joshua had banished his youngest child to her room for some misdemeanour or other it was Aunt Hepzibah who used to slip up with an apple or a slice of pie concealed beneath her apron.

'Today we address our very special prayers to the Lord for the safety of our dear sons,' Sir Joshua was intoning.

He stood behind the low table, his hands clasped over his black gown, his eyes raised. Ranged on stools before him were his three daughters. Grey-gowned with their hair tucked beneath white linen coifs they sat with their hands demurely folded, their eyes fixed on their father. Behind them stood the two kitchen maids, the cook who was fat and bad tempered, the two stable lads and Obediah, who was near sixty but as gnarled and tough as an old oak tree. Obediah made it his business to report to Sir Joshua on the behaviour of the rest of the household, a habit that rendered him exceedingly unpopular with everybody except Sir Joshua.

Several of the shepherds, the coachman and two gardeners had gone to fight in the cause of the Parliament. Since their going the household had been depleted of men and the women servants had been called upon to dig and plant and hoe.

'Lord God of Battles!' Sir Joshua was intoning. 'Defend us in this hour of peril when the forces of anti-Christ rise up against the legions of the righteous. Steel our hearts in the defence of all that we hold most dear. In particular, look with favour upon our beloved Elisha and Luther who, with other brave young men, fight in Thy cause!'

Aunt Hepzibah sniffed and dabbed her eyes with a handkerchief. She occupied a high-backed chair in the corner of the room and, like her brother, was dressed in black, as if Elisha and Luther were already dead.

Sir Joshua had not wanted his sons to go to war but, considering that it was his duty to set an example, had arranged for both seventeen-year-old Elisha and sixteen-year-old Luther to be signed into the New Model Army that was being formed in the eastern counties. They had left three months before but there was good reason for supposing them to be back in Yorkshire, for reports of the advance of Parliamentary troops were reaching even the remoter districts.

'Cast down the enemies of God to the pits of hell! Smite them with fire and sword and let their hopes crumble into dust,' Sir Joshua said.

Purity frowned slightly. Not for the first time it occurred to her that the God to whom her father prayed had grown, in her imagination, into a mirror-image of Sir Joshua. God had a pale face and a pointed beard and wore a black gown with a white collar. Probably all God's angels wore black gowns with white collars too.

'Do you find something *amusing* in this morning's prayers?' Sir Joshua demanded suddenly.

'No, indeed,' Purity said hastily.

'Then why were you smiling?'

'At the thought of victory,' she said brightly.

'Hm!' He gave her a doubting glance. 'I would have you remember that victory can only be gained by suffering and the garden of joy is reached along the path of sacrifice. Is that clear?'

'Yes, father,' chorused Hope and Mercy.

Purity said nothing. For just an instant the small room which was exclusively for prayers had looked quite different. The panelled walls had given place to white-washed ones and in the place where her father stood was a fierce, skin clad figure in a spiked helmet.

The impression lasted for no longer than the blinking of an eye and then was gone. She shivered a little, trying to listen sensibly to her father who had resumed his prayers to the Almighty.

Afterwards, however, when she was

in her room sorting out a clean pile of linen Aunt Hepzibah tapped on the door and stole in, closing the door behind her and lowering her already soft voice to a whisper.

'Purity, my dear, I must not delay your duties, but I could not help noticing that you seemed a little distracted during prayers. I do beg you not to make a habit of it or you will vex your father very much.'

'Aunt, is it true that another house used to stand here once, before Ladymoon Manor was built?' Purity cut in.

'Why indeed there was,' Aunt Hepzibah said. 'Did you not know that a Roman villa stood here many hundreds of years ago? When this house was being built the foundations of the Roman dwelling were excavated. Under the carpets in the prayer chamber is an original mosaic floor, but your father thought it too gaudy and so had it covered.'

'Romans living here.' She knitted her

smooth brow as if she were listening for the tread of long vanished feet.

'I believe most lived at York,' her aunt said, 'but there were undoubtedly settlements throughout the neighbourhood.'

'A tribe of savage men with horned helmets and painted faces attacked the house,' Purity said. 'The family who lived here were all killed and the house itself looted and destroyed.'

'Have you read something about it somewhere?' Aunt Hepzibah asked.

'It was something I seemed to know,' Purity said slowly.

'You must have read it in a history book,' her aunt insisted.

'Where would I find such a thing in this house?' Purity demanded. 'The only books father will allow are the Bible and Foxe's Book of Martyrs. And you know I cannot read or write well, for it was not considered seemly for Hope or Mercy or me to go to the Grammar School at York or even to the Dame School. Girls must be meek and mild and wait upon their betters.'

Her young voice had assumed a harsh, hectoring tone. Aunt Hepzibah gave one of her short bursts of laughter and then looked distressed.

'You must never mock your elders, my dear,' she said nervously.

'I never mock you!' Purity exclaimed, giving the older woman one of her swift fervent hugs. 'You are my dear, good aunt and I shall never understand how you came to be my father's sister!'

'Now that will do!' Aunt Hepzibah said severely. 'You must get on with your work and put undutiful thoughts out of your head.'

She wagged her finger and went softly out again, her own head shaking a little as if she saw what went on in the world and sought to deny it.

Purity hurried to get the clean linen into the high presses that stood against the walls. Hope and Mercy were in the kitchen helping cook with the preparation of the meals that would be consumed during the next few days.

Since the war had begun supplies had been difficult and expensive to obtain, and the household had been depleted of stocks of sugar, spices and the Madeira wine of which Sir Joshua permitted himself a daily goblet. Instead they made do with the honey from their bees, those garnishes that could be picked from the gardens, and an occasional bottle of cognac smuggled, at great expense, by the pedlar who came three times a year. Apart from those small inconveniences the struggle between King and Parliament had not, as yet, touched them. But now Elisha and Luther were with the Parliamentarians and might, despite their youth, be killed. Purity, laying the last pile of napkins down and sprinkling them with lavender, wondered if she would be very unhappy if anything happened to her brothers. It would certainly be her duty to mourn, but she was a little ashamed of not feeling more anxiety on their account.

When she had closed the presses she

went downstairs into the side hall and stood for a moment, listening to the voice of her father. He was evidently lecturing one of the maids for his level tones were punctuated by faint sobs. That must be Jessie who had a sweetheart over Otley way. Purity had seen them dallying in the orchard beyond the kitchen garden. Evidently Obediah had seen them too.

Purity went slowly into the main hall. The door of the prayer chamber was closed and would remain so until evening prayers. Sir Joshua did not approve of his family going in and out as they chose to the room reserved for God's business. Through the half-open kitchen door she could see her sisters, their fair heads bent over a large bowl of vegetables, their faces gravely intent. She watched them for a moment, wishing that she had their tranquil, unquestioning natures. Her own temperament was mercurial, storm and sunshine by turns with one or the other never far beneath the surface.

For the time being she was free from intrusion. She went swiftly into the garden that stretched lawns and rose bushes to the hedge that separated the grounds of the manor from the sloping moorland that fell away to the wooded river bank below. Among the clustering oaks over to the left were the crouching, ivy-clad ruins of the ancient convent.

Purity hitched up her skirt and went crabwise down the winding path. In this month of July the river leapt with trout, their fins sparkling through the translucent water that reflected the tangled rushes that grew thickly along the banks.

This was her favourite place, away from the confines of the house and the rules Sir Joshua imposed upon his family. By the leaping water, in the fastness of green willow and silver birch and brown oak, she was free to be herself. Not that she was certain what that self was yet, for it seemed to her that just when she had decided she was gentle her whole being was inflamed by temper and when she was angry at the whole world laughter would bubble up in her. But down by the river she could skip from mood to mood with nobody to frown or approve.

Convents, Sir Joshua said, were dens of iniquity, where young women of dreadful moral character lived and where, in the past, they had entertained monks of equally dreadful habits. Sir Joshua had never made it clear exactly what went on, but Purity, from hints dropped by the maids, had a vivid picture in her mind. Instead of shocking her the image she conjured up made her want to laugh, a wickedness of which she knew it was her duty to be ashamed.

On this bright morning her mood was, however, unusually subdued. The columns of stone, the creeper-hung walls, the broken arches of the ruined building roused within her a brooding melancholy. From a distance Elisha and Luther seemed more noble and more beloved than they had ever been at home, but her sadness was for all the young men who were fighting as well as her brothers. Sir Joshua had told her that a holy war was a glorious event in which God always triumphed. But if that were true, the girl thought, how very silly to begin to fight at all.

She sat down on a mossy stone resting her pointed chin on her cupped hands, letting the quietness of the wood wash over her. There was no noise save the babbling of the river and a scrabbling in the undergrowth just behind her.

Half turning, she gave a startled little gasp as a man crawled from the thicket and pulled himself upright. He was a tall man, grimy and unshaven, with sweat damp ringlets hanging about his face and tattered lace edging his dustsmeared suit.

'A Roundhead maid! My luck goes ill!' the man exclaimed.

Purity, forgetting her fright in indignation, scowled at him. She hated the nickname 'roundhead', for it reminded her of the wooden doll that the pedlar had once given her. The doll had painted black eyes and tufts of black hair and she had loved it very much, but after Obediah had caught her dressing it up in a bit of red woollen stuff and making it a little crown of gold tissue, Sir Joshua had taken it away, and thrown it on the fire, and held her to make her watch it burn. It had done so slowly, legs and arms dropping away into ash, until nothing was left but the little round head rolling in the glowing embers.

'My name is Purity, sir,' she said coldly. 'Purity Makin.'

'Makin? Are you Sir Joshua's daughter then?' A sharpness had entered his voice and he was looking at her with a new attention.

'The youngest, sir. I have two sisters and two brothers.'

'So your father was not averse to a little indulgence in the sins of the flesh! I confess I wondered how your mother would fare, for I guessed her marriage would be in a chilly climate.'

'Did you know my mother?' she enquired.

'Aye! In our green days we went a-maying together — but you talk as if she were dead.'

'When I was born, sir, thirteen years since.'

'Yoni dead!' he exclaimed. 'Yoni Marchmont dead and I never knew of it. But then I've spent most of the last twenty years in the south. Little Yoni Marchmont!'

'Makin, sir.'

'I knew her before her wedding,' he told her.

'You do not look so very old,' she said politely.

'Next spring I will be forty, but I feel nearer seventy,' he said wryly.

'Have you been in battle, sir?'

'James Rodale at your service.' Too weary to bow he sketched a salute with his battered hat.

'And there was a battle?'

'Do you live on the stars and moon in this place?' he enquired. 'There has been fighting all around York these past two days, and yesterday we met at Marston Moor.'

'My sister swore she could hear gunfire,' Purity remembered, 'but my father said it was only thunder and bade her curb her foolish imagination.'

'Is he not away at the war?'

'He is past fifty, sir, and opposed to violence, but he thought it his duty to send my brothers to support the Parliament.'

'Are they of an age to fight?'

'Not really, sir, but my father says God is on our side.'

'I imagine that is exactly what Sir Joshua Makin would say, being safe within his own four walls,' James Rodale said grimly. 'Well, I've seen cannon and shot and I tell you that God, if He exists at all, has no interest in our petty squabbles.'

Purity stared up at him in horror, waiting for some sign of wrath from the Being he had just denied, but the calm peace of the summer afternoon still enfolded them.

'You are a King's man?' she said nervously.

'For my sins.' He gave a brief laugh that hinted at selfmockery. 'I have sought advancement at Court for many years and scarce come within sniffing distance, but I fight for that little stammering man who is our King.'

'You look,' she frankly, 'more as if you were running away.'

'Because Fairfax and Cromwell between them hemmed us in and cut off our return into York. The Roundheads hold the city now and much joy may it bring them!'

'Then our side did win,' she began and stopped short, remembering that it was not godly to mock a fallen foe.

'A battle is not a war,' he said grimly, 'but must we argue out the time with talk of conflict? I'd give my soul for something to eat and a pint of — whatever Roundhead brew is to hand.'

'I can get meat and bread and ale,' she said helpfully.

'And not tell your father?'

She shook her head.

'My father would think it his duty to hand you over to the Parliament troops,' she said.

'And you would not?'

'For my mother's sake. She'd have wished me to aid a friend.'

'That's true,' he agreed. 'She was a sweet-natured lass.'

'You will have to wait here,' she told him. 'It may be dark before I can get out of the house again. As it is I'll be well-scolded for neglecting my duties!'

'I don't suppose you could provide a mount? My own was sore wounded and died beneath me.'

'I dare not. Obediah sleeps above the stables, with one eye ever open for thieves. He bolts the door from the inside.'

'But you'll bring food?'

25

'As soon as I can,' she promised, rising.

His hand reached out and fastened upon her shoulder.

'You'll not betray me?' he said, low and tense. 'Long years ago, when my hopes were still high, and your mother and I dreamed of cherries in November — for the sake of that shall we vow friendship now?'

She hesitated, looking up into his tired face, and then held out her small hand and placed it in his own.

'I'll not betray you and you will not betray me,' she said, her pointed face lit by a smile that made her suddenly enchanting.

He had withdrawn into the thicket by the time she had reached the foot of the path. For an instant she hesitated, then sped up the winding path to the gate in the hedge.

As she came up to the door her eldest sister ran out to meet her. Hope's face was even paler than usual, her eyes so red-rimmed that Purity thought for a moment she had been punished for something or other. Her words however clarified the situation.

'You're to come at once to bid father goodbye. Eben just arrived with word that Elisha was wounded a day since over at Marston Moor. He and Obediah are riding to York at once to see how he fares! And you with your gown all rumpled!'

'What of Luther? Is he hurt too?'

'Eben says he stayed with Elisha to wait father's coming. Do hurry, Purity, or we will both be in trouble for delaying the going.'

She pushed her young sister ahead of her to the parlour where Sir Joshua, already booted and spurred, was tying on his cloak.

'Your gown is crumpled,' he said at once, his cool eyes flicking her. 'Remember that cleanliness is next to godliness.'

'Yes, father,' she said demurely.

'Hope has told you of your brother's being wounded? Eben fears it may be a grave hurt, so Obediah and I ride at once to York. I charge you to behave properly and not give me cause for displeasure.' He gave her a long, frowning look.

'No, father.' Purity clasped her hands together and asked, 'Will Elisha get better, do you think?'

'I am no prophet,' Sir Joshua said grimly. 'His age and good health will be of help in his recovery, and I can ensure he obtains the services of a competent apothecary. For the rest we must pray that it be the Lord's Will he should recover.'

'Will you be gone for very long?' Hope asked.

'If he is well enough to travel we will return at once, but I will try to send word. You will not neglect your prayers or your duties, I trust. Where is Mercy?'

'Aunt Hepzibah is greatly distressed so Mercy brewed her a tisane.'

'Your aunt has no strength of character,' Sir Joshua remarked, jamming on his hat. It boasted a silver buckle and a green feather but it was so modestly decorated in comparison with popular fashion that Purity was moved to exclaim, 'If you run into any of the King's men they will take you prisoner for sure.'

'Nonsense! They would have no interest in a private gentleman. You will not alarm your aunt further with such notions, do you understand?'

Purity bobbed a curtsy. It was, she knew, exceedingly wicked of her but, with her father and his steward gone, it would be a simple matter to give a horse to the man who hid down by the river. If it were God's Will that her brother should be hurt this was the most convenient time for it.

Sir Joshua was bending to kiss them. She offered a submissive cheek and trailed after him to the door again.

Obediah, also cloaked and hatted, had brought round the horses from the stables and was already mounted, a stout cudgel in his hand. As Sir Joshua climbed to the saddle Mercy hurried to join her sisters. Of Aunt Hepzibah there was no sign, presumably she was too distressed to appear.

'Stay near to the house and be sure to bolt the doors and fasten the shutters. I dislike leaving females in charge, but hard times cry out for desperate measures. Pray often for your brothers and commend yourselves to the protection of the Most High.'

He raised his hand and cantered around to the back from whence a wide path meandered towards the distant walls of York.

'Do you think Elisha is very badly hurt?' Mercy was asking, her blue eyes wide with apprehension.

'He's young and strong,' said Hope, echoing her father.

'We'll have to pray very hard,' Mercy said.

'But we must make certain that Aunt Hepzibah is feeling better,' Hope reminded them. 'She is apt to become very nervous, you know.'

Hope, at fifteen, would be very like Aunt Hepzibah in another twenty years time, Purity thought. Recently, she had developed a habit of twisting her fingers together and ducking her head. And Mercy, at fourteen, was already a staid housewife.

'We will have to make sure the beds are aired and sweetened for when the men return,' she was saying now. 'Purity, come and help me to shell the peas.'

The day moved its accustomed hours towards sunset. It was a mark of Sir Joshua's character that even in his absence the work was still done as carefully as if he were watching, and not even Aunt Hepzibah, racked by nervous headache, would have dared to suggest missing evening prayers.

Purity found it even more difficult than usual to keep her mind on the words. After prayers the servants retired to their beds in the loft over the kitchen, the two stable lads had pallets in the grain barn and cook a room to herself behind the pantries. Aunt Hepzibah was safe for the night as soon as she had retired to her own chambers and Mercy and Hope usually sat in the parlour for an hour or so.

In the course of the afternoon she had managed to filch half a mutton pie, some cheese and a flask of cider, and these provisions, hidden in a small basket, were in the woodpile.

'I'll take a walk in the garden,' she said casually as Hope pronounced the last Amen.

'Father said we were not to stray,' Mercy reminded her.

'Only a breath of air.' Purity was sidling to the door. 'I'll be back long before we lock up.'

'Do be careful,' Hope begged. 'There may be soldiers about if there's been fighting.'

Purity had already gone. Unlike her sisters who remained indoors most of the time she preferred to be outside, a practice which Aunt Hepzibah declared would ruin her complexion. Pausing only to snatch the basket of provisions from the woodpile, she hurried across the long-shadowed lawns to the trees that fringed the river banks.

James Rodale was there, his attire even more crumpled than it had been before as if he had slept away most of the intervening hours. He began to eat at once, licking the crumbs of pie and cheese from his fingers, gulping cider.

Satisfied, he wiped his mouth with the back of his hand and grinned wryly.

'Hunger makes me forget my manners. I thank you, Purity Makin.'

'It was all I could contrive to bring,' she said shyly.

'After two days without victuals it tasted like a banquet,' he told her.

'It's possible for me to leave the stable door open too,' she informed him. 'My father and Obediah had to go away on — on business, so if you wait until dark there'll be nobody to hear.'

'No dogs?'

'My father has no liking for them.

There is a roan in the stall nearest the door. His name is Moonlight and he's biddable and makes good speed.'

'Your mount then?'

She shook her head.

'My sisters and I share him, but they don't care for riding, so he's more mine than theirs. I'll leave the door ajar before I go back in the house. Our two lads sleep in the barn and they're too careless to check the other locks. But you'll be very quiet?'

'As the grave in which I might have been laid if you had not taken pity on me,' he said. 'I will return the horse to you one day by some means or other.'

'Where will you ride now?' she asked.

'To Shrewsbury, to rejoin His Majesty's troops.'

'And fight again?' Her voice was small.

'And fight and win,' he assured her.

'I must go back to the house,' she said, 'or one of my sisters will come seeking me.'

'I have no family to care about my whereabouts,' he returned, 'but you will think of me, Purity Makin, won't you?'

'Yes, sir.'

As he leaned closer she wondered, half-fearful, half-hoping, if he were going to embrace her, but he merely pressed her hand and slipped away into the gloom of the encircling oaks.

Carrying the empty basket, she climbed the hill again without looking back, sped through the garden to the stableyard and, having left the door ajar, was in the big, stoneflagged kitchen when Hope entered.

'I'm just locking up,' the elder girl informed her. 'You look flushed! Is it colder outside now?'

'I hurried to keep warm,' Purity said.

'The fire in the parlour is kindled. Go and join Mercy. She has begun making bandages.'

'For Elisha?'

'He may need them when father

35

brings him home. Do as you're bade and stop dreaming,' Hope complained.

'I'm going now.' Purity bounced out of the kitchen, wondering if, with Sir Joshua gone, Hope was going to take it on herself to order them all about.

In the parlour Mercy was placidly hemming linen. Purity moved the candle nearer and drifted over to the window. The parlour and kitchen faced the front garden, but trees and bushes were swallowed up in the approaching darkness, and it was impossible to hear the murmuring of the river.

Leaning her head against the small, leaded panes she wondered how long it would take to ride to Shrewsbury and how many years might pass before James Rodale came back again.

2

Purity was singing, not very tunefully, a ditty that she had heard Jessie humming in the days when she ran to meet her sweetheart over in the orchard.

The lovers had been married now for more than a year and Jessie still hummed as she went about her work, for she had a cottage of her own and twin boys squalling in the cradle. Purity walked the three miles across the moor to see her as often as she could, but with the two stable lads away at the war the burden of work fell more and more upon those who had remained at Ladymoon Manor. Obediah now looked after the gardens and the horses with only a small boy, the son of one of the shepherds, to help. Cook and Lizzie managed the cooking and the rough work between them, and the Makin girls did the rest. Sometimes

Purity, sighing as she rubbed beeswax into the panelled walls or pounded rose-petals for one of Mercy's brews, wished it were for girls to ride to war and enjoy the excitement of conflict. Not that she approved of fighting, of course, she assured herself, but it would have been interesting to be in the middle of everything, knowing what was going on, instead of being stuck in the middle of nowhere with news coming in so slowly that it was often a month late before it reached them.

Today, however, she felt happy. It was August and the gardens were at their most luxuriant, the hedges spilling blossoms onto the thick grass, the river running high. The trees were weighed down with fast ripening fruit and against the south wall peaches clung rosily to their trellis of green.

What made her happier than the weather, however, was the fact that Sir Joshua had ridden to York, and Ladymoon Manor had an air of unaccustomed holiday. Obediah had gone over to consult Eben about the sale of some ewes and his absence added to the pleasure of the day.

It was a pity, she thought, raising her face to the blue sky, that Elisha had not lived to enjoy it. Two years had passed since her father had ridden back from York with the news that Elisha had died of his wound.

'It is not for us to question God's will,' Sir Joshua had said, 'but we naturally feel sorrow at the loss of our dear Elisha. I am told that he died bravely. Luther was with him at the end.'

Luther had remained with his comrades to fight on against the King. On the rare occasions he came home these days he seemed older than his years and graver even than his father. But there was hope that he would soon be home for good, for since the Royalist defeat at Naseby the King's men were widely scattered and most of the north was in Parliament hand. The King himself was in the north-west, trying to decide whether to rouse the Welsh to some action on his behalf or march against the Scots, but it was confidently expected that he would have to seek terms with Essex and Fairfax if he hoped to keep his throne. Sir Joshua brought back the London dispatches as soon as they were published in York.

Purity listened eagerly when he read them aloud to the rest of the family, wondering if the name James Rodale would ever be mentioned. The memory of that evening when she had hurried down to the river with a basket of food for him had stayed in her mind as the most romantic event that had ever happened to her. Sir Joshua had blamed the theft of the horse on his own foolishness in leaving the house in charge of a group of females. But Purity disregarding his grumbles, could think only of Moonlight with James Rodale on his back galloping along the Shrewsbury road. He had promised to return, but with the King's party so near defeat, she could not imagine how he could ever contrive it.

'Purity! Sister, where are you?' Mercy had come fussing into the garden, her hands pulling her coif straight as she ran.

'What's amiss? Is the house afire or has Aunt Hepzibah seen a mouse?'

'Luther is on his way. Hope just caught sight of him and another man riding towards the stables. I wish he'd sent word of his coming for there's nothing special prepared for supper and the jellies I made are not yet set.'

'He'll not notice what he's eating,' Purity said comfortingly, 'for the pleasure he'll take at sleeping in his own bed again.'

'Beds!' Mercy clapped an appalled hand to her mouth. 'I must go up and make certain the beds are aired. Will he expect a room of his own — the other gentleman I mean, or will it serve if I put him in with Luther? Purity! Why are you standing idle?'

'I'm going! I'm going!' Purity tugged her own coif into place and ran across the garden almost full tilt into the arms of her brother who, striding around the corner of the building, caught her and held her at arm's length.

'Greet me more gently!' he exclaimed, laughing. 'You attack as if you were one of Rupert's cavalrymen!'

'Give you greeting, my brother.'

She received his kiss and glanced shyly at his companion.

'This is Robert Masters. We are given a week's leave by command of General Cromwell but as Rob's home is in Cornwall I invited him here, the travelling being shorter,' Luther explained.

'Give you greeting, Master.' She bobbed a curtsy and offered her hand to the tall, slender youth in the green cloak and orange-ribboned hat.

'My sister is hoydenish though she is past sixteen,' Luther apologised, giving her a frown.

'You ought to come home, brother, and teach me manners,' she retorted.

'Where is father?' he demanded as

they went into the house.

'At York on business. He'll be home again before you return to the war.'

She stopped as Hope, her hands laden with lavender spikes, came from the parlour. Hope looked, as usual, anxious and timid as if she had neglected some duty and were about to be scolded for it. Her fair hair, curling about her temples, gleamed against her pale skin.

'My sister, Mistress Hope,' Luther said. 'Hope, this is my good friend, Robert Masters. Can you find room for us both for a day or two?'

'Indeed we can. Give you greeting, Luther, and you, sir. You don't bring bad news?'

She spoke in the soft, breathless manner that irritated Sir Joshua who called it 'twittering'.

'Good news, mistress,' said Robert Masters. 'The King's forces are scattered and he will have to sue for peace before many months have passed.'

'I am glad of it,' Hope said. 'We

are not much touched by the war here, save that poor Elisha died and Luther is absent from us, but we are constantly waiting for news of some battle or other.'

'Those who wait often suffer most,' Robert Masters said, 'but it helps those who must fight to know others are anxious on their behalf.'

'Robert has no family,' Luther said.

'Nobody at all?' Ushering them into the parlour Hope turned startled blue eyes upon the visitor.

'Which is why I make bold to hope that my friends are concerned for me, just a little?'

'Indeed, sir, we shall hold you in our prayers as if you were more than friend,' Hope said.

Purity, watching, thought, 'Hope's eyes reflect the lavender she carries and her cheeks are quite pink. Why, she is grown beautiful all in an instant.'

Later, under cover of the general conversation, she whispered as much to Aunt Hepzibah.

'Do you think so, my dear?' the older woman glanced at the others nervously. She and Purity sat a little apart from them, sorting wools. Mercy, who was never shy, was leaning forward in her chair, eagerly questioning her brother about the conditions of living under military discipline. Hope was darning a pair of stockings and said nothing, but frequently she would raise her eyes to steal a glance at Robert Masters, and each time she did so her cheeks flushed delicately.

'She is seventeen,' Aunt Hepzibah murmured. 'Seventeen is a very pretty age to be.'

'And you are from Cornwall,' Mercy was saying. 'I thought all Cornishmen followed the King.'

'No more than all Suffolk and Lincolnshire men follow Cromwell,' Robert Masters said. 'Protestantism is strong in the extreme west and even the most ardent monarchist fears the King's flirtation with Popery.'

'What is your trade, sir, when you

are not fighting?' Mercy asked.

'I had a small farm,' he told her. 'No more than fifty acres but the land was fertile and the house a good size. But I had ill-luck, for the wells ran dry in a drought summer, and taxes rose so steeply that I had to sell off a good piece of it. When the war began I leased out what was left and followed the drum.'

'Will you go home when the war is over?' Hope had broken her silence.

'I will reclaim my farm, mistress,' he told her. 'A Cornishman loves his land as he loves his faith and will fight to preserve both.'

' 'Tis a long distance off,' she said in a low voice.

'Aye, but worth reaching at journey's end,' he assured her.

There was a little silence broken only by the crackling of apple logs in the hearth. Even at the height of summer a fire was always lit in the parlour after dusk. It cast a cheerful glow over the dark wood of walls and furniture and the few pieces of tapestry that shielded those who sat there from draughts.

'Eight o'clock!' Luther broke the placid stillness. 'We must have prayers or the servants will never get to their beds! Aunt Hepzibah, you will ruin your eyes by screwing them up in such a fashion.

'It is growing darker,' she complained, glancing towards the window. 'There's a storm brewing, I think.'

'Don't say so!' Hope implored.

'Why, you are not afraid of storms, are you?' Robert Masters asked.

'Since she was a child,' said Aunt Hepzibah. 'When thunder sounded, were it ever so distant, she would run to her chamber and bury her head under a cushion.'

'Why, there's nothing so grand as a storm!' he exclaimed. 'To be snug within walls, listening to the thunder and the wind and watching the lightning shiver the sky! And when it's over with the trees dripping heavy, and the birds creeping out to praise the calm, and the moon flaunting high above the clouds! There's nothing like it, mistress!'

'It sounds like beauty,' Hope said, 'and not danger when you speak of it in such a fashion.'

'Beauty and danger are good comrades,' he assured her.

'As many gentlemen could testify,' Luther said, with unexpected joviality.

Indeed his natural gravity of manner seemed to have deserted him. He laughed more easily and even ventured upon a mild jest or two. It seemed as if his friendship with the young Cornishman made him more human. Purity, watching him as he stood in Sir Joshua's place to read the prayers, decided she liked her brother better than she had done when he and Elisha had gone everywhere with unsmiling faces like pale copies of the father.

By the time she and Mercy were abed the sky was quite dark with sullen streaks of lead outlining the rolling clouds. They had left the shutters open and a wind rising beyond the orchard rattled the panes.

'The storm is holding off,' she said, craning her neck to look beyond the lawns.

'Do get into bed,' Mercy pleaded. 'Your feet will be frozen if you stay there much longer. And do fasten the shutters.'

'I pity your husband when you find one,' Purity said crossly, banging the shutters and clasping the window. 'You will do nothing but fret him.'

'I don't want a husband,' Mercy said.

'But you cannot be an old maid,' Purity objected. 'Only ugly girls without dowries are old maids!'

'I'll wed when I have to, not before,' Mercy yawned.

Purity bounced into bed, her toes curling against the cool sheets.

'Do you think Hope likes Robert Masters?' she asked.

'Luther's friend? Why, yes, we all like him, I think.'

'I meant — in a special way. Do you think Hope likes him in a special way?'

'What sort of special way?'

'A marrying way!' Purity tossed back her plait of dark hair in exasperation. 'Do you think Hope likes Robert Masters in a marrying way?'

'It's for father to say whom we marry,' Mercy said placidly. 'Liking has nothing to do with it.'

'Do you think mother liked father?' Purity enquired suddenly.

'Whatever made you say that?' Mercy asked in surprise.

'I never remember father ever talking about her,' Purity said. 'Aunt Hepzibah told me once that mother liked to wander in the garden by herself. It sounded a lonely thing for a married lady to do.'

'Perhaps she liked looking at the flowers.'

'She was much younger than father. I wonder if they were happy together.'

'As happy as most folk,' Mercy said

placidly. 'What set you on this subject all at once?'

'Seeing Hope's eyes so blue and thinking we are nearly women full grown and of an age to take husbands.'

'Had you one for yourself in mind?' Mercy asked dryly.

'For myself? Heavens, no! We never go about to meet anyone, do we?' Purity said.

As the first long groan of thunder echoed across the hills she thought of Moonlight with the dust-streaked figure clinging to the saddle as horse and rider shortened the miles to Shrewsbury.

By morning the fine weather had broken and rain streamed steadily past the windows. Fires were lit in both parlours and the last bottle of cognac brought up at Luther's request.

'This is like Yuletide,' Aunt Hepzibah commented as they sat in the larger room late in the afternoon. 'Hard to believe there is a war on.'

'It will be over as soon as we have mopped up the remaining pockets of resistance,' Luther said, tilting his goblet. His face was slightly flushed, his eyes overbright. Luther was not accustomed to drinking overmuch, but with his father absent he prided himself on acting as generous host.

'You talk as if you commanded the entire Parliament forces!' Purity scoffed. 'Why, you're not yet nineteen years of age and there you sit, talking like a greybeard!'

'He always had an old head on his shoulders, even when he was a little lad,' Aunt Hepzibah said. 'Hope and Mercy were the same. You were quite different, Purity. Always into things as soon as you could crawl, never wanting to sit still.'

'I am tired of sitting still now,' Purity said, jumping from the low chair where she had been crouching. 'Cannot we play a game?'

'I always liked Spillikins,' Aunt Hepzibah said. 'I do believe we have a box of them somewhere or other.'

'Oh, not a sitting-room game!' Purity

begged. 'Let it be Hoodman blind or Kiss-in-the-Ring.'

'Hide-and-seek is a good game,' Aunt Hepzibah said.

'We cannot rampage through all the rooms,' Mercy objected. 'Obediah is in the kitchen and would have a fit.'

'Obediah is not master here,' Luther said.

'You'd have thought he was the way he grumbled when you brought up that last bottle of cognac!' Purity giggled.

'Hoodman Blind is a brave game,' Hope said.

'Is that the game you like best, mistress?' Robert Masters asked.

She nodded, a curl of fine, fair hair escaping from her coif. Her cheeks were pink again and between her parted lips her teeth showed small and white.

'Then let it be Hoodman Blind,' he said. 'Come, Mistress Hepzibah, we will use my sash to bind your eyes.'

'It is so many years since I played,' she began, but allowed herself to be blindfolded and turned around.

She caught Mercy, who in turn captured Hope, and Hope, crying half in fear, half in laughter, that she could not keep her balance, thrust her hand towards Robert Masters and was imprisoned in his grasp.

'Luther?' she queried, but her lips twitched with mirth.

'A forfeit, a forfeit!' Mercy clapped her hands. 'You must kiss her, Master Robert!'

He bent his brown head and for an instant they were a tableau in the dancing firelight, and then she broke away, pulling off the orange sash and laughing, as if she invited more kisses.

'Come, Robert, you must bind your eyes and catch you another lass!' Luther cried.

'I need no blindfold for that!' Robert retorted, and put his arm about Aunt Hepzibah, kissing her soundly.

'La, sir! You have me a-tremble!' Aunt Hepzibah giggled.

'Who shall be next to wear the

hood?' Robert Masters demanded.

'You cheated!' Purity accused. 'You have not yet worn it yourself!'

'Cornishmen are excused,' the young man began and stopped, his eyes fixed on the doorway.

Sir Joshua, cloaked and hatted with Obediah at his heels, stood in the side hall, the expression on his face of such forbidding severity that Aunt Hepzibah began to weep at once.

'I told you there were scandalous and evil doings, sir,' Obediah cried.

'That will do.' Ignoring his steward Sir Joshua came into the parlour and looked round at the flushed and excited faces. 'So you are home, Luther,' he remarked.

'For two or three days only, sir,' Luther said stiffly.

'And we must give thanks to the Lord that you are not sick or wounded. I wish I could thank Him for your conduct also, but you appear to have introduced gutterways into my household.'

'I am to blame, Sir Joshua,' Robert Masters began, but the other held up his hand, glancing towards his son.

'Will you not present your friend, Luther?' he enquired unsmilingly.

'Robert Masters, Sir Joshua, of Truro in Cornwall,' Robert said.

'You are a long way from home,' Sir Joshua said.

'Too far to travel in the time at our disposal,' Luther said. 'Truro is — '

'I am aware of the location of Truro,' Sir Joshua said. 'You are welcome, Masters, in my house, though I cannot welcome your roistering. I fear you have picked up evil habits on the march.'

'We were only playing Hoodman Blind, father!' Purity said crossly.

'With your brother Elisha only two years in his grave? I like not such disrespect for the dead!'

'I suggested Spillikins!' Aunt Hepzibah moaned. 'You would not have objected to Spillikins!'

'Hope, take your aunt to her room

and brew her a tisane or something,' Sir Joshua said. 'Mercy, take my outdoor things and see to their drying and bring my gown and slippers. Purity, I have been riding most of the day and need an early supper. Luther, where are you going?'

'N-nowhere,' Luther stammered.

'Sit down, both of you. I shall be interested in all the news you have to tell me. Be so good as to pour me a little of my excellent cognac — if there is any left.'

'Oh, indeed there is!' Luther said heartily.

'Purity, will you stop dreaming and perform your task,' her father snapped.

Purity followed her sisters and aunt who had already fled. In the hall she paused to draw breath, and to stick out her tongue at Obediah who, back towards her, was fiddling with the shutters, his ears pricked for any further gossip.

Sir Joshua had evidently decided to overlook the game he had interrupted for when they met for prayers he did not refer to it except for a remark to Mercy whom he advised to retire early to recover from her gaieties.

Two days later, under a showery sky, the two young men rode away. Purity, turning, caught the shine of tears in Hope's blue eyes.

'Come into the parlour,' Sir Joshua said from the main door. 'I wish to talk to you all.'

The three girls followed him obediently, only Hope pausing to cast a wistful look at the two mounted figures.

'You are no longer children,' Sir Joshua began. 'The time has come when we may begin to discuss the disposal of you in matrimony.'

They stared at him, their young faces blank.

'These are difficult times, but it behoves us all to live as normally as possible,' Sir Joshua continued sententiously. 'Birth and death and the giving in marriage must go on, and you cannot spend your lives at Ladymoon

Manor. That is why I recently went to York.'

'To arrange a marriage for one of us?' Mercy asked.

'For Hope, who is the eldest of you, should have the privilege of being wed first. Benjamin Rathbone is a very worthy gentleman, an acquaintance of mine whom I know, from experience, to be sober, industrious and honest. He has a small clothiers in Micklegate and plans to open another one soon.'

'How old is he?' Purity asked in a small voice. Hope was saying nothing at all but continued to gaze at her father.

'He is near forty, but has not, until recently, been in a position to take a wife. Now that his aunt who kept house for him has died he feels free to do so. He approached me very civilly and I agreed to the match.'

'But he has never seen Hope!' Purity exclaimed. 'How can he wish to marry her?'

'I assured him she was strong and

comely and modestly reared,' Sir
Joshua said. 'I trust they will find
great contentment together.'

'It is out of the question,' Hope said
in a shaking voice. 'I cannot possibly
wed this — this — '

'Benjamin Rathbone. You must not
imagine that I intend you to wed him
tomorrow! Now that he has spoken he
will visit us as your betrothed. I do
not anticipate a marriage before spring.
You will wish to sew your gown and
prepare yourself.'

'But I cannot!' Hope said desperately.

'I'd appreciate an explanation,' Sir
Joshua said coldly.

'I cannot marry,' she repeated.

'I have assured you that Master
Rathbone is a most worthy gentleman,'
her father said. 'He is also well-
favoured, not that handsome faces
are the least consequence, but I do
know that females take account of such
things.'

'I am sure he is a most considerate
and charming gentleman,' Hope said

breathlessly, 'but I cannot marry him, because I have already agreed to marry someone else.'

'Without my permission?' Sir Joshua now looked as stunned as his daughters. Purity, watching, felt an hysterical impulse to giggle.

'He intends to ask you when he comes here next time,' Hope said.

'Are you trying to tell me that you have already received a suitor under my roof?' Sir Joshua said.

'No, indeed I would never have thought of such a thing,' Hope said. 'I never thought of marriage at all, save as something that would happen a long time ahead in the future. But when we met we knew at once, without words. He would have spoken to you before he left, but I told him to wait. I feared you might think it too soon for us to know our own minds.'

'I am not interested in the state of your mind,' he said coldly. 'Am I to take it that you are referring to Robert Masters?'

'We knew at once,' Hope said eagerly. 'He is a fine young man, truly he is. He's young and strong and willing to work hard.'

'And might serve me well as groom or shepherd on those recommendations,' Sir Joshua said, 'but hardly as a son-in-law.'

'He has land of his own!'

'A few acres and a cottage in the barbaric county of Cornwall. He told me about it!'

'He would have every care for my comfort.'

'Do you think I would have none?' he enquired. 'I have a care for all my children. Luther will inherit Ladymoon Manor, but the three of you will have generous dowries and husbands who will keep you in moderate comfort. Benjamin Rathbone is not yet forty and is, while not a wealthy man, a reasonably prosperous one. You can have no quarrel with that.'

'I've never gone against you,' Hope began tremblingly.

'And you will not now.' Sir Joshua rose, dismissing them. 'Let us have no more nonsense about rushing off to Cornwall with a young man who, while he may be welcome as Luther's comrade-in-arms, can scarcely be considered as a prospective member of this family.'

'I'll not do it!' Hope sobbed when he had gone. 'I'll not wed this man from York even if he is the most suitable man in the whole country!'

'I don't see it makes any difference which one you wed,' Mercy shrugged. 'Marriage will be all cooking and sewing and having babies anyway. You'll be more comfortable doing that in York than in a place like Cornwall.'

'You don't understand,' Hope said. 'You've never fallen in love in your life.'

'Ah, well, I'm scarce sixteen,' Mercy said philosophically, 'so there's time yet. But if falling in love makes me as miserable as it seems to make you then I'll take care to avoid it. You'd better come and help me with the beds, Purity. Aunt Hepzibah is lying down with the vapours, having convinced herself that Luther is going to be killed.'

She glided out, slim and graceful and pretty, and unawakened, Purity thought, gazing after her.

'If Benjamin Rathbone comes to pay me court,' Hope sobbed, 'I'll lock myself in my room and stay there.'

'That wouldn't do any good,' Purity said sensibly. 'Father would only break down the door and drag you down. He'll not brook opposition!'

'If only Robert had known us before, or had land nearer to us,' Hope sniffed. 'Father would surely be reasonable if only we had a little time.'

'You have until spring,' Purity encouraged. 'If you're cool and distant to Master Rathbone — why, you could hint you've another sweetheart. A gentleman would have too much pride to force another man's betrothed against her will!'

'And in the spring Robert has promised to come back!' Hope wiped her eyes and looked faintly more cheerful. 'He may have earned a promotion by then, or done something very gallant that earns him the approval of the generals.'

'Will you write to him?'

'I shall write every day,' Hope said, 'but there is no way of getting them to him, so I'll save them up until we meet again, and then he can read how miserable I was while he was absent.'

'And you can sew your wedding gown!' Purity exclaimed. 'That will please father, and there's no need to mention who the bridegroom is going to be.'

'You make me feel better,' Hope said gratefully. 'One might think you in love yourself. You seem to understand exactly how I feel.'

'I'm like Mercy,' Purity said. 'I don't know any gentlemen. Are you feeling sufficiently better to go and help her with the beds, instead of me?'

'I'll help her.' Hope gave her sister a swift kiss and went, more jauntily, out of the room.

Purity glanced through the window, wondering if she could risk a swift walk in the garden, for the house stifled her, but rain still dripped from the leaves and a chill wind ruffled the lawns.

She went through into the hall and hesitated for a moment, trying to guess where her father might be. She was feeling angry with him, more angry than she had ever been even when he had punished her for some trifling fault. Hope had done nothing wrong, but Sir Joshua had calmly arranged for her to be wed to a man she'd never even seen, and when she'd told him of her love for Robert Masters he'd dismissed it as if it were of no consequence.

'We're not sheep to be sold to the highest bidder, or mated with the strongest ram,' she muttered, her face flushing with temper.

From the kitchen she heard Obediah

scolding the cook who answered briskly, tongue flashing fire. She and the steward were old enemies, and usually Purity enjoyed listening to their sparring. Today, however, she felt too indignant already, and there was every chance of Sir Joshua coming by and finding her some unpleasant task to do to humble her spirit.

Greatly daring she opened the door of the prayer chamber and went inside. The small room at the back of the main hall was used only during the morning and evening hours when the family gathered for worship. Sir Joshua would not allow anyone to enter it save at those times except for Aunt Hepzibah who cleaned it once a month. Certainly it was the one place in the house where one could be completely undisturbed.

The fire was laid but unlit in the small hearth and only a faint light came through the round window set high above the small table on which the prayer book and Bible rested. Everything in the room from panelled walls to dark carpet was sombre. Even the candlesticks were of plain wood. Purity, looking around, longed for some gold or silver to gleam and sparkle.

Aunt Hepzibah had said something once about a mosaic floor that had been part of the original Roman house. Purity knelt down and rolled back the closely woven carpet. The floor beneath was tiled in alternating squares of blue and gold, and patterned with stars and tiny flowers.

It was the prettiest floor she had ever seen, and Sir Joshua had covered it over. The anger within her grew stronger as she stared at the bright tiles. Her father, she decided, would cut down even the flowers in the garden if he had his way. In his world everything had to be grim and dark. Even the gowns that she and her sisters wore were of grey or brown stuff and Sir Joshua frowned when he saw their curls escaping from the confines of net and coif. And even these stars and flowers were, in his view, too gay.

Indignantly she pounded her small fist on the floor, finding some measure of relief in pretending it was her father's head. The tiles were chill and one echoed hollowly. Echoed and began to move.

She stared at the widening crack, and then, in sudden excitement, inserted her fingers and pushed gingerly. The tile slid beneath its companion, and a cavity, with something in it, was revealed.

Anger forgotten, she drew up the object and stared at it in wonderment. It was a cup, a twin-handled goblet of gold, so heavy that it was difficult to hold aloft.

Traced in silver on the side of the goblet was the face of a woman. Despite the gloom she could discern quite clearly the long-lidded eyes, the gently smiling mouth. The handles were snakes with silver tongues flicking from their downbent heads.

'You're beautiful,' Purity whispered. 'I wonder if you're Roman too.'

Roman or not, the cup could not have lain hidden since Roman times. The tile had slid aside too easily and there was only a fine film of dust over the gold. She blew on it gently and rubbed it with the corner of her sleeve.

It was warm in her hands and the longer she held it the more certain she was it throbbed as if some ancient heart were waking into life.

'You're my secret,' Purity murmured. 'I don't know if father hid you here, but I doubt it. You look as if you belong in a church, and he thinks gold church ornaments should be melted down.'

She put the cup back into its hiding place, slid back the tile and turned the carpet into place again. Everything was as it had been before, but some of the anger had been drawn out of her.

3

'It's no use,' Hope said, laying aside her needlework. 'I cannot even begin to enjoy his company or look forward to his coming. I find myself praying that the rain will keep him away.'

'Master Rathbone is a most godly man, my dear,' Aunt Hepzibah said nervously.

'But not as a husband for me.' Hope went over to the window and stared miserably at the sodden garden.

'At least you are spared his company at Yuletide,' Purity said.

'Only because he's gone over the border to buy two carriage horses,' Hope said, drumming her fingers on the sill. 'He's the dullest creature I ever met in my life. I've made it clear that I care nothing for him, but he gives me that dreadful, understanding smile and says all will come right when we are wed.'

'You have until the spring,' Aunt Hepzibah said. 'By then something may happen to change matters!'

'Nothing will happen,' Hope said gloomily. 'Master Rathbone will come back with the horses, and my gown will be finished and we'll be wed. What else can happen?'

Leaving her aunt and sister to talk Purity slipped from the room. Had she stayed longer she might have been tempted to blurt out the information she had been keeping to herself for more than two months.

It was the arrival of the pedlar that had given her the idea. Nathan had been coming by for many years, though in recent times his visits had been few and far between. But his cart and plodding pony had been sighted on the horizon as September waned, and it was then that the idea had leapt into Purity's fertile young mind.

While Aunt Hepzibah and her elder sisters discussed the merits of thread and ribbon Purity went up to her aunt's room and snatched paper and quill from the small table in the corner. Aunt Hepzibah only used paper and pen on the rare occasions when she needed to order something from York or wished to leave a note for the cook. Purity had never written to anyone in her life.

Hastily she scrawled in the slanting script that she had been taught,

Dear Master Robert Masters,
    They are forcing me to wed. I beg you to save me.
      Your good friend,
      Hope Makin.

Sanding it, Purity glanced doubtfully at the spelling. It didn't look absolutely correct, but there was no time to change it. Robert Masters had never seen any of Hope's writing anyway. She sealed the paper carefully and wrote Robert's name across it. After a moment's thought she added, 'Care of General Oliver Cromwell'.

Then, with it tucked inside her sleeve, she ran downstairs and let herself out quietly into the garden. Nathan had finished his business and came whistling out, his hat pulled over his eyes and climbed to the seat of his cart. As he jogged away Purity hurried to catch him up, waiting until she was out of sight of the windows before she called his name.

'Oh, 'tis you, Mistress Purity.' He reined in the pony and shifted round to look at her. 'I wondered where you could be, but the other ladies were too busy choosing the stuff for the wedding gowns for me to get round to asking after you.'

'Nathan, could you do me a favour?' she asked.

'What kind of favour? I can't afford to be giving away things free.'

'I don't want you to give me anything. I want you to deliver something for me,' she said.

'Deliver what?' he asked, still suspicious.

74

'A letter. A very private letter.'

'And where am I supposed to deliver this letter?' he asked.

'To a gentleman in the army.'

'Oh, that's rich!' Nathan chortled. 'A gentleman in the army. Which army had you in mind, mistress? There are two of them rampaging up and down the country, not to mention the Scots leaping over the border and the pesky Irish just waiting their chance to invade and make us all into Papists.'

'The gentleman is in Cromwell's army,' Purity said. 'He's a friend of my brother's. Couldn't you pass it on and ask someone to see that he gets it?'

'Love-letters, eh?' Nathan winked heavily and slipped the letter into his bag.

'You'll not lose it?' she said anxiously.

'No, and I'll not go running after the entire army either, instead of carrying on with my business,' he said sourly. 'Times are hard and my profits this year won't see me through the winter, but I'll do what I can, if I run into any Parliament men.'

That had been two months before and since then there had been nothing. For all she knew the letter had been lost or destroyed by now. There was certainly no guarantee that it had ever reached Robert Masters.

The door of the larger parlour was thrust open and Sir Joshua said sharply, 'Purity, are you idling as usual?'

'Yes, I mean, no. No, father.'

'Call down your aunt and your sisters. I want to speak to all of you.'

'Mercy's in the kitchen.'

'Then I'll get her myself, but call down the others. I have something important to tell you.'

'Is Luther — ?'

'Call them down, girl, and don't add chatter to the vice of sloth,' he said irritably.

A few minutes later the four of them were gathered in the parlour under Sir Joshua's eye. He had taken his seat behind the low table and stretched between his hands a document from which an orange ribbon dangled.

Purity's heart gave an uncomfortable little leap. For one awful moment she thought it was the letter she had written and braced herself for the explosion of temper that would surely follow.

Sir Joshua, however, was looking at Hope. 'It seems,' he remarked, 'that I underestimated Master Robert Masters. He has obtained permission to wed you from General Cromwell. Modern manners, it seems, are not what they were in my youth. In these days the prospective bridegroom does not trouble to ask his sweetheart's father for permission to wed. He goes instead to his Commanding Officer, who in turn approaches his own Superior. And a letter is written.'

'From General Cromwell?' Hope's face matched her name.

'From Cromwell's private secretary. It addresses me civilly by name, and informs me that General Cromwell is pleased to grant leave to Robert Masters to travel into the county of

Yorkshire to be married to Mistress Hope Makin.'

'You'll not refuse me now?' Hope pleaded.

'It would never do to offend General Cromwell,' Aunt Hepzibah whispered.

'Were it a matter of conscience,' Sir Joshua said, 'I'd offend any man without fear or favour. What is the opinion of men compared to the opinion of God?'

'But if you offend the General,' Purity said shrewdly, 'Luther might be the one to suffer for it.'

'Does the letter say when Robert is coming?' Hope asked.

'On the seventeenth. He will bring a minister and a licence with him. Apparently he leaves nothing to chance,' Sir Joshua said drily.

'The seventeenth is tomorrow,' Mercy said. 'But her gown is not hemmed and no cake is baked,' Aunt Hepzibah fluttered. 'I wish we had received word earlier.'

'The dispatch rider who brought it

had been on the road for three weeks, and had other letters to deliver,' Sir Joshua said.

'Gowns and cakes matter nothing when the man is the right man,' Hope said softly.

'You are certain of your mind?' Her father looked at her intently.

'Completely,' she said, with a ring in her voice that Purity had never heard before.

'I've a mind to hold back your dowry,' he said, 'and see if Master Robert would take you without it.'

'He would take me with nothing save the gown I wore,' she returned. 'Cannot you understand how it was, father? We knew as soon as we met that it was meant. I could never be happy with any other man.'

'And what of Benjamin Rathbone?' Sir Joshua demanded. 'He too expects to be a bridegroom.'

'Why cannot he take one of the others?' Aunt Hepzibah said brightly. 'It never seemed to me that Master

Rathbone had any great partiality for one or the other of them. He merely wishes for a wife.'

'I had not expected such intelligence from you,' her brother approved. 'He can wed Mercy instead, for her dowry is the same, and in looks she is very similar to Hope.'

'He mates us like animals,' Purity thought, the anger rising up in her again. Mercy, however, said tranquilly, 'As you please, father, though I'd not looked to be wed so soon.'

'You're sixteen and healthy enough for childbearing,' Sir Joshua said. 'We can only pray that it will please Master Rathbone. There is no way of letting him know in time of the change in plans.'

'You are not angry, are you?' Hope asked.

'I am not happy,' he said coldly. 'If it were not for the fact that Cromwell himself approves the match I would forbid such an unequal affair. Robert Masters has very little to offer and his influence upon Luther is not the happiest. I saw a certain coarseness and levity in my son's behaviour that did not please me.'

'But you will not forbid it?' Hope said.

'I've given my word.' He frowned slightly as he rose. 'If there is a gown to be hemmed and a supper to prepare, you, none of you, has time to gossip.'

'Don't you mind being wed to Master Rathbone?' Purity enquired curiously of Mercy as they sat together later, working on the gown of creamy wool that Hope would wear.

Mercy shrugged her graceful shoulders.

'I don't think of it one way or the other,' she said. 'I told you before that I always expected to have to be married one day, and Master Rathbone will do well enough. We shall be living in York, too, so father may allow you to visit us. Poor Hope will have to go into Cornwall.'

'She won't mind,' Purity said confidently. 'She loves Robert Masters.'

'Has romantical notions about him, you mean!' Mercy exclaimed. 'I sometimes think I am the only one with commonsense. There! Do you like it?'

She held up the finished dress. Plain save for a sash of deep blue to match the blue coif, it had a charming simplicity.

'She will look beautiful!' Purity cried. 'You're a fine needlewoman.'

'Because I apply myself to the task in hand and don't go moonshining,' Mercy said.

'Do you think father would allow a few flowers?' Purity asked. 'Oh, I know 'tis not the season, but there is some pretty silver fern down by the river.'

'Put on your boots,' Mercy advised, 'or you'll be kneedeep in mud down there.'

Mercy was always so practical.

Dragging on her boots, Purity wondered how her sister could bear to live without dreams of love and cloaked figures riding out of the mist.

Rather to her surprise as she squelched down the path beyond the hedge she caught sight of Hope, cautiously reaching for a spray of rowan.

'The berries are so pretty,' the older girl said as Purity joined her. 'And they do say rowan protects one from witches, not that I believe such heathenish superstitions.'

'There are silver ferns, too,' Purity said. 'They would mix well with the red and the green of the rowan. And they might serve to keep witches away at that!'

'Plants cannot ward off evil,' Hope objected, 'and I have no fear of witchcraft.'

'You look as if you have no fear of anything,' Purity said.

'Not since the letter came from General Cromwell,' Hope said. 'I could not have thought up such a scheme that would make our marriage possible so soon!'

'Gentlemen must be very clever at managing things,' Purity said demurely.

'Robert is,' Hope said serenely.

'Are you so sure of him?' Purity asked with sudden misgiving. 'It was so short a visit you'd scarce time to be alone together.'

'If we had never even spoken,' Hope said, 'I would still have known that I wished to marry him. It sprang up between us. I cannot explain it to you, but one day you may know something in yourself of what Robert and I feel.'

Into Purity's mind sprang the picture that had come often in the past two years. The tired man with the sweat-stained hair whose deep voice echoed still in her ears had become with the passing of time not more shadowy but more deeply etched.

'Cornwall is a long way off and barbarous,' she said aloud.

'No more barbarous than any other place, I'll wager,' Hope declared. 'When the war is over Robert will take me to his farm, and we'll make a home together.'

'The ferns are plucked.' Purity held

them up. 'Set the rowan berries against them. Oh, but they look gradely! Father cannot mind if they are tied into a modest bunch.'

'He has been very fair-minded,' Hope said judicially. 'I was so afraid he would forbid me still, even after he'd read the letter to us, but he was very good.'

'Because he fears that Luther may lose his chance of promotion,' Purity scorned, 'if he refuses his permission after the General has approved.'

'I wish you could get on with father,' Hope said. 'You and he have never been close.'

'Nobody has ever been close to him, in my opinion,' Purity said.

'He is a very private man,' Hope said charitably. 'But I am so happy that I want all the world to be happy too!'

'You must have been unhappy,' said Purity, 'believing you would have to wed Benjamin Rathbone.'

'I have been most bitterly unhappy,' Hope said quietly. 'You cannot imagine how it has been, to have to sew my dress and choose stuff for my travelling cloak and, all the time, pray that father would relent, or Master Rathbone alter his mind, or that some other miracle would happen. I don't know what I would have done if the day had actually arrived and I had found Master Rathbone waiting for me with the minister!'

'You would have surely refused to make your vows,' Purity said. 'I know I would.'

'Ah, but you are different from Mercy and me,' Hope said. 'You never would accept what life gave you, even when you were a very little girl. You would argue and fight and break your heart against stones.'

'And you will wed Robert Masters,' Purity said, 'and need never wonder if I could ever have found the courage to refuse Benjamin Rathbone.' Hope said, 'I'm glad he's to have Mercy. She will make him a good wife, and he will like her quite as much as he would have liked me. I wish that you had someone of your own.'

'I shall choose my own husband,' Purity said, 'so father need not trouble himself.'

'And we'd best get back to the house,' Hope reminded her. 'This mud clings to everything.'

'The river is swollen,' Purity remarked. 'And there is more rain up in the clouds.'

'I want a final fitting for my gown and coif,' Hope decided as they toiled up the hill again. 'Is your new dress ready?'

'I think so. I'd have liked a red one, but Aunt Hepzibah almost had the vapours when I suggested it, so Mercy and I are wearing — '

She had paused, her hand above her eyes as she peered through the drizzle.

'What is it?' Hope enquired.

'They're here,' Purity said. 'There by the door, I can see Luther and — '

'Robert!' The ferns and sprays of

rowan were scattered as Hope, her usual dignity forgotten, picked up her skirts and ran across the lawn.

Purity, feeling immeasurably more sensible than her sister for the first time in her life, stayed to pick up the leafy sprays. Hope must truly be in love to drop everything and run as she had run.

The rowan and ferns secured she went to join the others. Hope had gone indoors but Luther stayed where he was, staring at the puddled ground.

'Give you greeting, brother!' She put her hand out, but he didn't seem to notice it.

'Brother? Are you at odds with me before I've said two words to you?' she demanded. 'Or was it — are you angry because of the letter? I wrote it, not Hope.'

'I recognised your hand,' he said, 'as soon as I saw the letter.'

'Hope doesn't know. You'll not tell?'

'No. No, I'll say nothing,' he promised.

'Luther? Luther, what is it?' she asked, for he had spoken almost automatically, as if his thoughts were miles away.

'Robert is — he was killed a week ago in a skirmish just outside Shrewsbury,' he told her.

'Oh, no!' She whispered the words. 'It's not true! You came early, that's all.'

'I brought the notice of his death,' Luther said. 'I was there when they brought in his body.'

'Poor Hope!' Purity's young face was drained of colour.

'Father and Aunt Hepzibah are telling her now,' Luther said. 'We'd best go in to them.'

Mercy was there too, crying bitterly like her aunt. Sir Joshua was pouring wine and his hand shook so violently that the neck of the bottle rattled against the goblet. Only Hope, sitting in a high-backed chair, displayed no grief. The expression on her face was one of mild interest as her father said, 'You must drink some wine, my dear. This has been a shock for you, I fear.'

'A dreadful, dreadful shock for us all,' Aunt Hepzibah sobbed.

'I cannot pretend that I approved of this marriage,' Sir Joshua said. 'I was willing to countenance it, and I would have treated Master Robert Masters with the courtesy due to a son-in-law, but I cannot say that it pleased me. However, I wished the young man no harm. I never would have wished him harm.'

'Why doesn't he stop talking?' Purity thought in anguish. 'Hope isn't listening.'

'Drink the wine,' Sir Joshua was continuing. 'We must accept this as the Will of the Lord, my dear. It is hard now, I realise, but in a little while you'll see more clearly that everything is for the best.'

'What happened?' Purity asked Luther.

'He rode out to reconnoitre a farmhouse which we suspected might contain Royalist snipers,' Luther said.

'It was an hour's task, no more.'

'And he did?'

'Robert was shot down. The trooper who rode with him brought back his body,' Luther informed them. 'But you don't know the worst of it yet?'

'Can there be worse?' Hope spoke for the first time.

'I was the one ordered to search the farmhouse,' Luther said, 'but I had a report to write for Colonel Ireton, so Robert offered to go in my stead. Had I thought the risk serious I would have refused, but the farmhouse was not ten minutes ride from the camp and they were only going to spy out the land. He said he'd be back to drink a mug of ale with me before the hour was up.'

'You can't blame yourself,' Mercy said warmly.

'No, I do not, for it could easily have been the other way with me receiving the bullet marked for Robert, but the fact is there. He died in my stead.'

'Did he — ?' Hope's voice trailed away.

'Through the heart. It was very quick,' Luther said sombrely. 'We buried him and a detachment of us razed the farmhouse. We had no other satisfaction for the King's men had gone.'

'Such a terrible thing to happen!' Aunt Hepzibah rocked a little in her grief.

'He had made a will,' Luther said. 'I didn't know it but he had left his Cornish farm to me. I suppose that after his marriage he would have changed it, but he was killed too soon. We were close comrades from the time Elisha was killed.'

'At least we must be thankful that Benjamin Rathbone knows nothing of this,' Sir Joshua said. 'Now the original arrangements can stand.'

'Arrangements?' Luther looked at him enquiringly.

'I forget you are not aware of events that have happened in your absence,' Sir Joshua said. 'A very worthy gentleman of York offered for Hope and I accepted on her behalf, though somewhat against her will. When the General's letter came today we decided that Master Rathbone should have Mercy instead. As he is away we have not had time in which to inform him of the decision, and now the need has gone for, with Master Robert dead, Hope is still free to wed.'

'Father, you cannot!' Purity burst out.

'My dear child, this is a sad affair but one must be practical,' he returned. 'Hope was ready to marry Master Rathbone before.'

'Only because she thought there was no chance of her being allowed to wed Robert Masters. And, at the last, she might well have refused.'

'Hope knows her duty,' Sir Joshua said, 'and would not shame me in such a fashion.'

'And have my sisters no choice at all?' Luther demanded. 'Surely, we must consider their feelings, sir!'

'My son, when you are older you

will learn that the feelings of females ebb and flow like the tide,' Sir Joshua said. 'Consider them too tenderly and you've a task for life.'

'Father,' Mercy began.

'You are disappointed at having your own chance snatched away? I can understand that, but you will have other opportunities. I'm minded to bring the wedding forward. Master Rathbone will be here with us after Yuletide and I'll put it to him then that there's no reason for delay.'

'I have a headache,' Hope said. 'May I go to my room?'

'Naturally you're upset and need a little time for grief.' He patted her shoulder. 'We will all grieve for the young man, but you must be brave and look ahead to next year when you will be a married woman with a comfortable home of your own.'

She had risen silently. Now she curtsied, her face tranquil, took the bunch of ferns and rowan from Purity's unresisting hands, and went out.

'You cannot seriously intend to marry her off to this other man!' Luther exclaimed.

'Within a few weeks she will have settled into an acceptance,' Sir Joshua said. 'Mercy, this is probably a disappointment for you, but there will be other gentlemen.'

'And what of Robert?' Luther said. 'Is he already forgotten now that he is dead?'

'We will remember him at prayers tonight,' Sir Joshua said. 'You will stay for a while?'

'I am to ride back to camp at first light,' Luther said.

'We will have an early supper. Hepzibah, surely you have better things to do than sit and weep!'

'Aunt will help me to prepare the supper,' Mercy said, drying her eyes.

'Good child!' Sir Joshua approved. 'Purity, you should take example from your sister.'

'Better than taking example from you!' Purity cried.

95

Anger and grief combined within her to burst into a fountain of words that gushed out of her as if they had been dammed up for years.

'You never treat any of us as if we were real people, with hearts and minds of our own! You never care what we feel, or trouble to find out what we want! And I won't have it so! Not for me!'

'Purity, be silent!' her father exclaimed.

'I won't be silent! I'll speak my mind,' she said.

'Then you may speak it where it won't trouble others. Go to your room at once.'

'You will make Hope wed Master Rathbone even when she loved Robert Masters so well; and Mercy will be married off to some other man, I daresay. But you'll not dispose of me so easily. I'll not be sold to the highest bidder, or have my life undone in the space of a few hours! I'll not wed until I choose, and when I choose nobody will stop me or marry me off elsewhere!'

She finished with a burst of angry tears and dashed headlong out of the parlour, heedless of muddy footprints.

Her tap on Hope's door was ignored, and when she tried the handle the door was locked. She went on into the room she shared with Mercy and slammed and locked her own door. Through the blur of tears the room shimmered dark and dismal like something glimpsed under water.

She sat down on the end of the wide bed and sobbed loudly and defiantly. It would serve her father right if she stayed here for ever and starved to death. But he probably wouldn't care anyway. He cared little for any of his family, but he had never loved her at all.

It had begun to rain heavily again as if the sky competed with her. Imperceptibly her own tears dried and she leaned back against the piled coverlets and slept.

It was dark when she woke to a rapid tapping at her door. Her eyelids felt heavy and scratchy, and her head ached.

'Purity, do let me in, my dear,' Aunt Hepzibah was pleading.

'Go away!' Purity sat bolt-upright, trying to rekindle her anger, but there was an emptiness in her.

'I brought you something to eat. Oh, do open the door before Joshua finds out.'

Purity unbolted the door and took the tray from her aunt.

'Joshua has said you're to stay here until supper tomorrow,' Aunt Hepzibah said. 'He said that hunger would humble your spirit, but I couldn't bear to think of you being hungry, so I poured some cider and put a slice of cake on a plate. It was the one we baked for the wedding. Cook was going to ice it, but there's no need for that now.'

'Father is cruel,' Purity said, looking at the cake. 'He's cruel and horrible and I hate him.'

'It was always so,' Aunt Hepzibah said. 'He'll never change, and it does no good to oppose him. No good at all!'

'Is Hope still in her room?'

'Best not to disturb her,' Aunt Hepzibah advised.

'It's monstrous!' Purity cried. 'To talk of her wedding another man so soon!'

'I was in love once,' her aunt said. 'Long ago when I was very young, and quite comely, though you might not think so now. But this young man wished to pay court to me. It was no use, of course. My father was in bad health and it was my duty to nurse him. The young man said that he would wait for me.'

'What happened?' Purity asked, her attention caught despite herself.

'My father died, and Joshua sold our London home and came up to York. He bought this house and he married your mother.'

'And what happened to the young man?' she persisted.

'My dear, I never knew. He may

have come back but by then we'd moved, you see. It was a very long time ago and I forgot him very quickly as Joshua said I would. I must go down or I'll be late for prayers.'

She gave her habitual nervous little bob of the head and crept away.

Purity closed the door and took her supper over to the window. Her intention of starving herself to death was forgotten in her hunger. Temper had always sharpened her appetite and she bit deeply into the fruity cake.

The rain was easy and the dark sky was lit by the rising moon. It hung against the curtain of the evening like a brilliant silver ball that some child had tossed up in play. In the garden below the trees and bushes were tipped with pale moonlight and when Purity opened her window a little way she could hear the rushing of the swollen river.

Perhaps Aunt Hepzibah was right, and all this, like the river, would pass. Robert Masters would be forgotten, as her aunt's suitor had been, and she and Mercy would wed, as Hope was constrained to do, according to Sir Joshua's desire.

'There is no escape,' Purity muttered, and was filled with a rebellious confusion of feeling.

Someone had come out into the garden. A slim figure, white as moonbeam, stole within view and stood, poised like a dancer, on the grass. Purity drew back, but Hope was not looking towards the house. She was looking up at the moon as if she were reading some message inscribed across its brilliant face.

She must have slipped out while the others were at prayers, treading softly that she might not be heard. And she was wearing the gown of cream wool that Purity and Mercy had finished hemming earlier that day. Its blue sash looked black in the moonlight, as did the coif from beneath which her long fair hair streamed over her shoulders like rippling water.

As she turned Purity saw the sprays of fern and rowan berry glinting in her hands. She had bound them into a bouquet and she held them proudly.

'Hope.' The younger girl whispered her name, but no sound reached the figure below. Only the river beat ceaselessly against its banks below the hill.

Hope began to walk slowly across the garden towards the white gate that glimmered in the high hedge. She moved with infinite grace, her head high and the bouquet in her arms, as if it were her wedding day.

'But she goes to a cold bridgroom,' Purity thought. She clung to the sill, her gaze fixed upon the moonlit garden, and the slim bridal figure moving through the gate.

For Hope there was, after all, escape of a kind, and perhaps the river, receiving its own, would be kinder than life had been. It was, thought Purity, a very private way to die, and not even a loving sister had the right to forbid it.

4

Purity had just returned from a visit to her sister's home in York. She rode there with her father or Luther in the summer and stayed for a fortnight while the sheep and horse markets were in high fettle. Luther had been home for nearly two years and shared with Sir Joshua the responsibility of buying and selling livestock and grain, but he had never really settled back into civilian life.

'Luther will not sit down and talk to me for longer than two minutes,' Mercy complained. 'He is forever wanting to be off somewhere else. I wish he would take a wife, but he finds nobody to his taste, though I'm sure that Benjamin and I have introduced him to at least half-a-dozen suitable young women.'

Mercy had been wed for four years to Benjamin Rathbone and could not complete a sentence without dragging in his name. The marriage that had begun in the shadow of Hope's death had gone well, so well that Purity suspected that Mercy loved her husband better than she liked to admit.

Certainly he was very kind to her and her house was comfortable.

Purity's first visit to York had been a time of enchantment. She had been fascinated by the bustling crowds who thronged the narrow streets, and the shops with their bulging, tiny-paned windows, the tall spired churches had been exciting. It was true that the people were soberly clad with no feathers or jewels, that no luxuries were on sale and that the churches had been stripped of all their ornaments, but to be away from Ladymoon Manor for a while with its memories was such a relief that she had enjoyed every moment of her stay in the city with conscious pleasure.

Her subsequent visits had never recaptured that first excitement, but the summer trips had become an annual pleasure, a brief period of escape from the bleakness of her life.

'You ought to be married yourself,' Mercy had said. 'Father would not object if a respectable gentleman were to offer for you. I'm surprised that he hasn't already arranged a marriage for you.'

'I am too useful at home,' Purity said drily, 'especially since Aunt Hepzibah began to fail.'

'I'd like to see both you and Luther settled,' Mercy remarked in the faintly patronising tone of a woman whose own life is securely content.

'Time enough yet. I'm scarce twenty,' Purity said. In her own heart she was not certain that she wanted a husband at all. She doubted also if anyone would want her as a wife, for she had none of her sister's placidity. Despite two miscarriages Mercy had never grumbled about her childlessness or wished for more than she had. Purity, watching her as she moved serenely about her kitchen, with an apron round her slender waist, decided she could never achieve such tranquillity.

She was not even certain that she wanted to, for in her mind still, as clear as if it had been imprinted there, was the tired man in the feathered hat and stained cloak riding along the Shrewsbury road.

'Are you idling again?' Sir Joshua's voice broke into her dreaming.

'I'm arranging flowers, father.' She held up the bowl to show him.

'A waste of the Lord's time,' he commented sourly. 'Where is your aunt?'

'Upstairs, lying down.'

'She spends half her life lying down these days, and she is ten years younger than I am,' he exclaimed.

'She's always seemed the same age to me,' Purity said. 'But she is not well, you know. When she tries to hurry her breath comes short and she complains of pain in her arm and chest.'

'I will bring the apothecary back with

me from York,' he said.

'Are you riding there again?' She looked up in surprise. 'Luther and I only just returned.'

'Having sold the sheep and wool at such a low profit that I might as well have given them away. I am riding over with Obediah, to find out how they contrived to cheat my son.'

'Luther's over at Otley, hiring two maids and a new shepherd.'

'And will promise them double the rate if I am not there — but I cannot be in two places at once. And I need Obediah in York.'

'Does Mercy know that you're going?'

'I made up my mind to it only an hour since. You're not suggesting that I need to seek Mercy's permission before I visit her?'

'I'd never venture to suggest anything to you, father,' she said coldly.

'You've a sharp tongue. It's the mark of an old maid,' he returned.

'Are you offering me a husband?' she enquired.

'It's your present duty to take care of my household until your aunt is recovered,' he said swiftly. 'When Luther returns you may tell him that I've gone to York to look into his business methods there. He has not even troubled to enter sale documents into my accounts file. I assume there'll be duplicates of them in York, but I shall have to track down the buyers. It annoys me terribly.'

'Luther hates having to sell grain and buy sheep,' Purity said. 'He wanted so very badly to remain in the army.'

'When Charles Stuart was executed and the Commonwealth established it was my son's duty to come home,' Sir Joshua said.

'But the King's son has invaded,' Purity argued. 'The Scots have crowned him at Dunbar.'

'And been massacred by Cromwell's troops.'

'Luther wished to join them,' Purity said. 'In York I suppose his mind was more on that than on sheep or grain.'

'He ought to concentrate his mind on his duties,' Sir Joshua said. 'The Royalists gained a little support in the north and since the rout at Worcester they have been hunted fugitives.'

'But Luther was going to fight for Parliament again,' she objected.

'The odds were so overwhelming that one more could have made little difference.'

'But Luther wanted so very much to go.'

'Luther has already done his duty to his country. From now on he'll do his duty to his home and family. I've told him, and I don't intend to argue it out all over again with you.'

He went out again, his heels ringing on the stone floor of the passage. Purity jammed a rose into the bowl and scowled at it. The seven years of war, she thought, had changed her brother from a solemn copy of his father to a restless, dissatisfied young man who yearned for the freedom and comradeship of the life he had learned to enjoy. But Sir Joshua had no sympathy or understanding.

She took the flowers up to Aunt Hepzibah, who lay on the day-bed in her small sitting-room. Her aunt spent nearly all her time up in the little, panelled apartment, reading over and over a book of poems that had once belonged to her when she was young. When she was not reading she was working on an immense bedspread which would probably never be completed, for she had a habit of undoing much of what she did in the belief her stitches were too large.

'Father and Obediah are riding to York,' Purity said. 'They've gone to find out where Luther sold the sheep. It seems he didn't make a profit handsome enough to please his lordship!'

'You mustn't talk like that about your father,' Aunt Hepzibah said unconvincingly. 'Your father has a right to expect Luther to take an interest in the running of affairs.'

'Why should he take an interest in something he's not interested in?' Purity said indignantly. 'I could run this place with father if he'd allow it, but in his view females are good only for cooking and sewing and making preserves. And Luther, who wants to travel, must be confined here.'

'We must learn to be content. Mercy learned the lesson. Mercy wed a man who'd been promised to Hope and took her as second best when Hope died.'

'He's very kind to her,' Aunt Hepzibah said, 'and he has never blamed her for having lost those babies.'

'She didn't *lose* them. They died before they were born,' Purity said angrily. 'Why should there be any blame to Mercy or to her husband? And why should Benjamin Rathbone be so highly praised, simply because he hasn't blamed Mercy for something that wasn't her fault anyway?'

'My dear, you sound quite fierce,' Aunt Hepzibah said nervously.

'I'm in a bad mood today,' Purity

said. 'Will you come down for supper tonight? I don't suppose Luther will be back until tomorrow.'

'I'll have something in my room,' the older woman decided. 'You'll not be lonely?'

'Not in the least,' Purity assured her. 'I'm in far too bad a humour!'

But she was lonely all the same and there was a bitterness in her admitting to such a state of affairs even to herself. Girls of twenty, she decided resentfully, ought to wear beautiful gowns and dance. Her own dress was of sober grey and Sir Joshua would rather see her dead than indulging in such a heathenish abomination as dancing.

In her father's absence it was her duty to conduct the evening prayers. She hurried through them and dismissed the servants, aware that she was safe in skimping her duty because Obediah had accompanied Sir Joshua.

By now they would be almost at the gates of York, and Mercy, with no diminution of tranquillity, would cook a meal and prepare beds for two unexpecting guests. Fortunate Mercy with her shining house and her kind husband who never blamed her for having miscarriages! Mercy's modest desires had been amply fulfilled. And Hope had chosen to go where desire no longer had any meaning.

'But I,' thought Purity, wandering out into the garden, 'am full of a hunger for something not yet satisfied.'

The long blue shadows of a September evening drifted across the river. Nobody from the house ever came down to the reed-fringed banks and the clustering trees that guarded the ruins of the despoiled convent. But Purity still loved the river in its moods, and when she thought of Hope it was not with the shrinking of those who fear the dead, but gently as one thinks of an absent friend.

She wandered down to the brink and knelt there, her hand troubling the placid water. It was peaceful here, with the manor house resting proudly on the hill behind her, and the moors purpled with heather. If she were a man she could ride out across the hills to discover what she truly wanted, but the water, grown still again, showed her a woman's face with dark eyes and a mouth that craved experience.

'We seem to make a habit of meeting in this place,' said a deep voice from behind her.

She knew who it was even as she turned for, in the years since their brief meeting, he had been locked in her mind.

'Master Rodale.' She scrambled to her feet and curtsied.

'And you are the Roundhead maid. I've not forgotten you.'

'Nor I you,' she said, and was afflicted with a sudden shyness that brought the blood into her face and set her fingers twisting her long skirt. 'Are you — are you escaping again?'

'We are all escaping,' he said wryly. 'You have been told of the battles?'

'At Worcester? Yes.'

'It was a rout,' he said gloomily. 'I could not have believed that history would repeat itself so soon. Last time it was the Martyr King and now 'tis his son, Charles the Second.'

'We have no King,' she said stiffly. 'We have a Parliament to rule now.'

'To rule! To sit and squabble while the land falls into anarchy you mean! God help us all when *Parliaments* rule.'

'King Charles was a very wicked man,' Purity said.

'Obstinate, vain, sometimes treacherous,' he said, 'but he was a King, and he died the death of a hero and a martyr.'

'And now your loyalty is to his son?'

'Who wanders with a price on his head and no shelter from his enemies, save that afforded him by the faithful few at the risk of their own lives.'

'He ought to have remained abroad,' she said sullenly.

'An exile king at a foreign court?

If you lost something that you prized wouldn't you seek it with all your strength?'

'I suppose so.'

'Of course you would!' he said heartily. 'And if King Charles came here you would not betray him.'

'I cannot tell,' she said helplessly.

'You would not, for I know you better than you know yourself.'

'Why, how can you?' she asked.

'Because you're a woman, my little Roundhead maid,' he said teasingly. 'A pretty woman too. A little beauty!'

'I thought that the Royalists had fled south,' she said.

'They are scattered in every hamlet,' he told her, 'but I came north. I can take ship from Liverpool.'

'But doesn't this take you out of your way, sir?' she asked in surprise.

'I had a fancy to walk this land once more before I leave it,' he said.

'My horse? I don't suppose you brought my horse back?'

'The poor beast has been dead of a

fever these three years,' he regretted. 'I am sorry for that. I broke my promise.'

'No matter. You have a horse now, I see.' She nodded towards a handsome sorrel cropping the grass at a few yards distance.

'I bought it with the ring my mother gave me when I came of age.' He spread his hands to show their lack of ornament.

'And she is dead?'

'Long since. Neither she nor my father lived to see the war.'

'If you have no money, how will you buy a passage on a boat?' she asked.

'I will smuggle myself aboard,' he told her.

'My father and his steward have gone to York, and Luther is over at the hiring and won't be back until tomorrow,' she said quickly.

'You're alone?'

'Aunt Hepzibah is sick and confined to her room, and the servants are in their quarters.'

'And it grows darker.' His teeth gleamed white in his tired face.

'We could slip in and upstairs to the room where Hope used to sleep.'

'Hope?'

'My sister who died four years ago. Her room is empty now. I could bring you food there and put fresh blankets on the bed.'

'A night's rest in a soft bed. It sounds pure bliss!'

'You are welcome to come, sir,' she said, and was shy again.

'Why would you take such a risk for me?' he asked.

'You told me that you knew my mother, and that she was gentle. She'd not have turned an old friend away. I never knew her, but I know that much.'

'Your nature is your mother's nature,' he said. 'I am tempted by your offer.'

'We can go along by the hedge and slip through the door. The servants will be at the back. What of your horse?'

'I've secured the beast to the tree.

It'll serve until morning,' he said carelessly.

'Come with me then. Tread softly and don't talk.' She put her finger to her lips and led the way up the hill towards the shadow of the hedge.

The main door still stood ajar. She pushed it open cautiously and peered within. The door into the kitchen was shut but she could hear the murmur of voices within. Evidently the maids were still clearing up. She turned to the right, slid back the panel behind which the concealed staircase would up into the large bedchamber where Sir Joshua slept.

James Rodale, obeying her beckoning finger, stepped within and she slid the panel back into place, and opened the kitchen door.

'Leave the cleaning until the morning,' she told the two young girls, who raised startled faces from the long table they were scrubbing.

'Cook'll complain if this isn't clean for the baking,' one of them said.

'Cook isn't mistress here,' Purity said briskly. 'Go up to your rooms and leave me to lock up.'

'Is it safe for us to be here with all the men away?' the other enquired.

'Tim and Nat are in the stables,' Purity reassured them, 'and there's no danger at all.'

'Not even with Royalists all over the country! They say that the King's son can leave no woman alone.'

'The king's son is a fugitive and won't have time at the moment to bother woman chasing,' Purity said. 'Anyway, he's probably many miles away by now, so leave this and get to your beds.'

They withdrew, looking faintly disappointed by the reassurances they had been given. No doubt the prospect of a lecherous young king excited rather than terrified them.

She moved swiftly, locking the doors, banking down the fire, bringing meat and bread and a large portion of apple pie from the pantry. With these and a jug of cider on a tray she hurried back through the hall, up the main stairs and down the corridor to the room where Hope had slept.

It was clean and neat, unused since Hope had crept out of it in her wedding dress to keep her tryst with the cold river. Purity set down the tray and lit the candles. With one of them in her hand, she crossed to her father's room.

This was the largest bedroom, its walls panelled, its hangings dark. The locked chest in which her father kept his money stood in one corner. Every month its iron-bound lid was lifted and the servants paid. In another corner stood the tall desk at which Sir Joshua sat working on the accounts with Obediah at his elbow. Another door opened onto the narrow staircase that led to the panelled entrance hall below. She opened it and looked down at the man who sat there, his chin sunk on his palms.

'Master Rodale,' she hissed. 'You

can come up now.'

'In faith, but I began to fear I'd sit here for ever. 'Tis wondrous dusty!' he exclaimed.

'These stairs are never used,' she said. 'There's a space under the top step big enough to hold a man.'

'You're not expecting me to occupy it!'

'You'll be safe in Hope's room. My aunt sleeps at the other side of the house and the walls are very thick anyway.'

He had risen and was looking down at the step with an odd, brooding expression on his face.

'This is where my father sleeps.' She indicated the sombre apartment.

'The panelling has lasted well,' he commented. 'The tapestries have been thrown away, I suppose, being in such bad condition?'

'Tapestries? There was never any in this room,' she began, and looked at him sharply. 'You talk as if you knew the house,' she said.

'I came here once, many years ago, when your mother and I were no more than boy or girl,' he said as they went out into the corridor.

She motioned him into Hope's room and stared at him.

'You and my mother came here? When? Why?'

'Twenty years back.' He tossed aside his hat and cloak and indicated the tray. 'Have I your leave to eat while I talk?'

'Yes. Yes, of course.' She hastened to pour cider.

'But you said you came here once with my mother?'

'And two other friends. We rode out for a picnic. I told you life was gayer then.'

'It must have been.' She tried to imagine what her father would say if she suggested going for a picnic.

'We rode out to this house. It was empty then — abandoned since the death of the last owner. Yoni was afraid of the place.'

'And in the end she wed the man who bought the house! Did you see her again after her marriage?'

He shook his fair head. 'I went down to London to make my fortune,' he said wryly. 'I fear my tastes were always too expensive for my means however. My father was a prosperous lawyer. He always hoped I'd follow him in his profession, but I had no liking for dusty documents.'

'If you had wed my mother,' she said. 'I might have been bred a Royalist.'

'Such a terrible fate,' he teased. 'But your mother would not have had me. She wed Sir Joshua instead, and came to Ladymoon Manor. I wonder if she was happy.'

'Nobody could be happy with my father,' Purity said. 'He's cold and hard, with no feeling save for profits.'

'A canting Puritan,' he said, 'but need we talk of him, or of the past? It was long ago when we were young and gay with the king safe on his throne.'

'You are young now,' she said, a

little pucker of anxiety between her brows.

'Past forty.'

'That is the prime of life,' she said gravely.

'When you say so I am inclined to believe it,' he said. 'Little girls tell lies so charmingly.'

'I told you once that I would never betray you,' she said, 'and I did not. I tell you now that I will never lie to you. And you don't seem old enough to have ridden to a picnic with my mother, for she died when I was born and that's twenty years back.'

'An eternity for you! Well, I still have my hair and my teeth and with God's grace I'll live another twenty years!'

He laughed and stretched, drinking the last of his cider.

'Your boots are all mud!' she exclaimed. 'If you'll allow me to pull them off I can clean them for you.'

'I will allow no such thing,' he said, 'but I'll take off my boots and coat if you've no objection. I must cut a shabby figure.'

'At least you'll not be taken for a Royalist.' She sat on the edge of the bed, feeling a delicious intimacy growing up between them as he stripped off his coat.

'Don't believe it. Every down-at-heel fellow is a Royalist these days,' he told her.

'I wish I had some money,' she said wistfully, 'but the chest in my father's room is locked, and if I took anything else one of the servants might be blamed.'

The golden cup had flashed into her mind, but it was too cumbersome to smuggle aboard a ship. And Sir Joshua must surely go, as she went, to look down at the gleaming bowl with its silver-tongued snake handles and the woman's face smiling into the dark. If he found the cup gone, if he guessed his hoard had been discovered, his anger would be terrible.

'I'll probably work my passage

somewhere or other,' James Rodale was saying easily. 'Or I'll slip across the border into Wales, and from thence take a ship to Ireland, and from Ireland the wind's set fair for France.'

'What you really mean,' she said in a small voice, 'is that you have no plans, and when you leave here I will know nothing of where you are or even if you are still alive.'

'Will it trouble you?' he asked, and his voice was gentle.

She bowed her head, clasping her hands tightly together.

'So! I didn't realise I had made so much impression on you. I thought you would have been married and settled.'

'I've sworn never to wed where I cannot love,' she said very low.

'And you've reached twenty without casting your eyes favourably upon any handsome young men? There must have been some young gentleman who took your fancy!'

'No, sir.'

'Never to have been in love!' he mused.

'I didn't say that, sir,' Purity said on a little gasping note.

'You say a great deal by the way you avoid looking at me,' he said. 'Your mother had the same shyness.'

'I'm not my mother,' she said, looking up at him. 'I'm myself. I'm simply myself.'

'And beautiful.' He came over and bent, cupping her chin in his hand. 'Did you know that, Purity Makin?'

'I never heard it said before,' she whispered. 'Is it true, sir?'

'I'll prove it.' He bent lower, imprisoning her mouth with his own. She would have put up her arms but he had stepped away and his voice was rough.

'I'll not have you bedazzled by soft looks and fair words,' he said. 'You'd best go to your chamber, Roundhead maid, before I forget my manners.'

'I could — stay,' she said with

hammering heart. 'I would be very willing to stay.'

'You're an innocent! Respectable woman don't make such offers.'

'This is not a worldly matter,' she said. 'It is a question of feeling, sir.'

'And you have such feelings?'

'And would be true to them, sir.'

She was looking at him with her heart in her eyes, her hands clasped so tightly that the knuckles showed white.

'You don't know what you're saying,' he said. 'Women do not give themselves to men in such a way. Those who do are not those whom men choose to marry.'

'I'd take that chance,' she said in a low voice. 'And there are many women who marry and never know the joy of giving themselves freely.'

'You're a child.'

'Past twenty, and you told me I was beautiful.'

'And spoke the truth.' He came back to her and bent lower. 'You are more lovely than your mother ever was, my dear. But generosity can be regretted, and in the years to come, when I am gone, you may blame yourself for offering, and me for accepting.'

'If you have no liking toward it,' she began, and was interrupted by his urgent, questing mouth.

'No liking!' she heard him mutter as his arms enfolded her. 'Dear Lord, but if you believe that you know nothing about men like me at all!'

'The candle, sir.' Her own voice shook between laughter and tears. 'Do pray blow out the candle.'

The darkness covered them and it was quiet save for the panting breaths of those who explore the secret flesh of a desired stranger. Purity had not known the reality of what she craved and the reality was better than the half-formed images of love that had sped through her thoughts.

Pleasure, she decided, as her own flesh warmed into his was a feeble word to describe the high ecstasy that quivered along her nerves.

'You must have had many women.' She tried to discern his expression through the darkness.

'Some.' His deep voice mocked a little. 'Did you believe I learned all this out of books?'

'My sister fell in love,' Purity confided, 'but her man was killed, and my father planned to wed her to another. But she drowned herself in the river. I thought I understood why she did such a thing, but I never really understood it until now.'

'You'd never do such a thing, would you?' he asked, faint alarm creeping into his tone.

'I doubt it, but then nothing is going to happen to you. I know that as surely as I know that I'm lying here. You'll get away safely and one day you'll come back to me. You will come back, won't you?'

She raised herself on her elbow and looked down at the long shape stretched beside her.

His hand, reaching up, tugged at her long dark hair. 'Yes, little Roundhead,' he said. 'I'll come back, when the young king returns, but it may be years yet, and when I do come you'll not want me.'

She scorned an answer for he was no longer a stranger but flesh of her flesh and she could not imagine ever growing tired of him.

In a little while, he slept, the blankets flung loosely across him, but Purity felt more awake than she had ever been. Her body tingled and she was acutely conscious of her own shape, as if she had just discovered what her lover had woken into being. Poor Hope, who had died without knowing this! Poor Mercy, who had been satisfied with less, for surely Benjamin Rathbone could never have inspired in her sister such a tumult of desire!

Stepping across the room she opened the shuttered window and looked out across the moonlit orchard. The leaves of silver quivered and there was a faint throbbing in the air as if the heart of the world beat steadily.

There was a louder throbbing now, from a different direction. Leaning across the sill and craning her neck towards the stables she saw the black silhouettes of two men on horseback.

'Father and Obediah? Riding back already from York?' She had uttered the words aloud, and James Rodale stirred and spoke. 'What is it? What's amiss?'

'My father and his steward are returned.'

Fumbling for clothes and candle she spoke jerkily, her voice ragged with panic.

'Bolt the door behind me. When I come back I'll tap three times, but stay close. If you are discovered, sir, we are both as good as dead!'

5

When Purity reached the foot of the main stairs she was confronted by her father, travel-stained and untidy. Obediah was presumably seeing to the horses for there was no sign of him.

'You're up late,' Sir Joshua said curtly.

'I couldn't get to sleep,' she said, 'and I was going to make myself a tisane. Did you change your mind about going to York?'

'We've ridden there and back. Is Luther home?'

'No, father. We don't expect him until tomorrow — later today.' She corrected herself after a glance at the clock which showed her it was already morning.

'Bring me something to drink into the parlour,' he said, 'and bind up your hair.'

'Is something wrong? Is Mercy sick?' she asked anxiously.

'Mercy is well enough. Where's your aunt?'

'In bed and asleep. Did you want her?'

'Leave her be. I'll have some of that pigeon pie with my drink, and tell Jessie to return to her bed. She heard me coming and rose to unbolt the door, but she'll not be fit for work later if she doesn't get her sleep. Be quick, girl.'

Tying back her hair as she went Purity hurried to the kitchen where Jessie was sleepily mulling ale.

'Is it a plague or an invasion, mistress?' she yawned. 'The master said nought but looked thunder.'

'I don't know. Get to your bed again and I'll finish up here.'

'Mistress Mercy isn't sick, is she?'

'No, no. My sister's well and in fine spirits.' Hoping it was true Purity bustled the maid up to the loft and went back to her task. Sir Joshua,

135

she thought gloomily, could not have arrived at a more inopportune moment. Not only was James Rodale still in Hope's room, but she herself had been torn abruptly from the contemplation of an exquisite experience. She should have had time to rest and dream of warm flesh and wake in her lover's arms. Instead she was down in the kitchen, mulling ale and cutting a wedge of pigeon pie for her father.

He had stirred the parlour fire into a blaze when she returned and was staring into the flames moodily. To her surprise he nodded towards a chair and said, 'Pour a drink for yourself and sit down.'

'You're troubled?' The word was not the right one, for the line of his mouth told of a cold anger rather than anxiety.

'I rode to York,' he said flatly, 'and Benjamin Rathbone greeted me with news I could scarce credit. He'd been on the point of setting off to see me, but Mercy had persuaded him to wait until daybreak. It's fortunate she did, else we'd likely have missed each other on the way.'

'What happened?' she asked.

'By chance Benjamin was talking to a local merchant who complained the price of my wool had been high this year. Benjamin was puzzled because the last time we met I'd confided what poor profits Luther had made. So he went further into the matter, made a few discreet enquiries.'

'And?' Nursing the mug of steaming ale between the palms of her hands she looked across at him anxiously.

'I stayed in York for less than an hour,' he said heavily. 'Benjamin had obtained copies of the original sales documents. There's no room for doubt. Luther pretending to me he'd failed to make good profits, sold at an inflated price and kept most of it for himself.'

'Oh, surely not! There must be some mistake!'

'The only mistake has been mine in trusting Luther,' he said grimly.

'I ought to have checked the sales documents, but I left them in his hands. I hoped to give him some sense of responsibility by so doing. He has repaid me ill.'

'By how much?' she asked in a small voice.

'By close to two hundred sovereigns.'

'That's lot of money. What could he want with it?'

'A question I intend to ask him as soon as he returns, I've left instructions with Benjamin who'll inform the magistrates.'

'The magistrates!' Purity looked at him in horrified surprise. 'You wouldn't hand him over to the Law, would you?'

'I'd hand over any who tried to rob and cheat me.'

'But Luther is your own son! He'll be sent to prison. He could even be hanged!'

'If he were twice my son,' Sir Joshua said coldly, 'I'd do what I've done.'

'Perhaps, as he stands to inherit

anyway, he simply helped himself to a little in advance,' she pleaded.

'He will inherit nothing,' he said. 'I'll not have this estate going to a thief.'

'But you must give him another chance,' she begged. 'At least let him explain!'

'There's neither explanation nor excuse for theft. It does you credit to think kindly of your brother, but it argues little for your good sense. Get back to your bed now. We'll have to be up betimes for I've no doubt Benjamin will arrange for a constable to ride out here to escort Luther back to York.'

Her mind was working furiously, but she kept her face and voice calm.

'I promised Jessie I'd ride back home with her. You know she's only been sleeping here as a favour until Luther came back with the new hirings.'

'I expected her to wait until they arrived,' he frowned.

'She's anxious about the baby. Her Mother's looking after him but he's fretting with his back teeth, so she wanted to get back.'

'With escort. She gives herself airs,' he said sourly.

'She's nervous of riding alone with so many Royalists wandering about the countryside, but I can send one of the lads with her.'

'No, I'll require them to be here. You'd best ride over with her yourself,' he said impatiently.

'If you say so.' She bowed her head submissively.

'Leave these things and go to bed,' he said. 'You'd best be off early with Jessie. I'll want you back by the time Luther returns. Your Aunt Hepzibah will screech and cry, no doubt, when the news is broken to her. Good-night.'

'Good-night.' She hesitated, wondering if she dare risk a further plea on her brother's behalf, but Sir Joshua was a man who, having made up his mind, would resist any attempt to make him change it.

She dared not take the risk, either, of

tapping at Hope's door lest her father came up on his way to bed. James Rodale would have to possess his soul in patience until she had leisure to smuggle him away. At least there was small chance of anybody trying to get into Hope's room. It had been unused since her sister's death and Purity was the only member of the household who entered it occasionally to dust. Her father never went near it. Although Hope's death had been passed off as an accident, and her body respectfully interred at York, the family could not have avoided mentioning the truth of it among themselves. Mercy had wept bitterly and then dried her eyes and set herself to the preparations for her marriage with Benjamin Rathbone. Sir Joshua had remarked icily that Hope must have run mad and he trusted neither of her sisters would go the same way, and had barely mentioned her name since. If Luther were truly guilty he could expect no charity from his father.

She slept fitfully, dreaming of James Rodale who was running away from her across the moor. In the dream she caught him up, tugging at his sleeve, but when he turned he had her father's face.

At dawn she dressed and went down into the kitchen where Jessie was already clearing the top layer of grey ash from the grate to expose the glowing heat beneath.

'Father says you can go home today,' Purity said. 'No need to wait for the hirings are due back with Luther sometime. I'll ride with you so put on your cloak and I'll have Nat saddle a couple of ponies.'

'I'm not dismissed, am I?' Jessie gave her a bewildered look.

'Dismissed? Of course not. Why should you be?'

'I cannot think of a reason, but with the master coming back from York so fast and in such humour I smelled something in the wind.'

'There's nought to smell,' Purity said

briskly. 'Be quick now.'

It was good to be in the open. The air was fresh and sweet with the slight crispness that heralds autumn.

Jessie's cottage lay three miles south of Ladymoon in the direction of Otley. Her mother's house, where her children were staying, was half a mile beyond. Jessie had twins now as well as her first boy, and from the thickening at her waist looked as if she were expecting again. When Purity mentioned it, she blushed coyly and giggled.

'My man enjoys his pleasure, and it seems the Lord made me fertile,' she confided. 'After this next one is born I've a fancy to stay at home and mind it.'

She sounded content, Purity thought wistfully, and wondered if Jessie still felt the tumult of passionate feeling that every woman in love must surely experience, or if, settled in marriage, her desire had dwindled to a mild affection.

They reached the house without

incident and, having seen Jessie reunited with her plump babies, Purity refused an offer of breakfast and rode on, leading the pony the maid-servant had ridden.

She had only visited Otley once in her life but it was not far distant and she knew the route her brother always took. She rode slowly, for though she was aware of the need for haste some part of her still dreamed of what had passed between her and Master Rodale in Hope's darkened bedchamber. At all sides lay the purple slopes, rising and falling to the horizon. She had, it seemed, the richly imagined world of the Creator all to herself, and such was its beauty that, forgetting present trouble, she reined in the ponies and sat, eyes half-closed, breathing in the perfume of the heather under the morning sky.

The next instant the bridle was seized by alien hands and she opened her eyes in terror upon a group of men who had risen from the high heather and now encircled her.

She had forgotten the gypsies who, in the course of their wandering, made yearly camp over Otley way. They were a small tribe, constantly pursued by the Law, disliked and feared by the shepherds and farmers whose livestock was never safe from the thieving hands of the dark eyed Boswells.

'Let me alone!' She thrust about her with her crop, but the man holding the bridle snatched it from her and flung it into the heather. He was no older than herself with mocking eyes and greasy lovelocks hanging about his thin, brown face.

'Two good horses, lady.' His speech was slurred and there was wine on his breath.

'They are my father's horses,' she said loudly. 'If you try to steal them he'll have you hanged for it!'

'If her dad's so powerful,' an older man observed, 'he'll pay good money to have his daughter safe.'

This threat was truly alarming. She looked about the circle of dark faces in terror.

'She wears no jewels,' another of them said. 'Clad in grey she be, like a sparrow.'

'The jewels are under her skirts, tied round her pretty thighs,' said the lad who clung to the bridle. 'Let's up her off her perch and find out.'

Purity took one horrified look at his thin face with its glinting upcurved eyes and smiling mouth and opened her own mouth to scream.

'What holds up the men?' A woman's voice, sharp with authority, rang through the air.

She was a tall woman, riding her mount astride, her long legs encased in breeches, a tall crowned hat shielding her brown face.

As she drew nearer the men fell back a little, their faces respectful.

'We found two horses,' one of them said.

'Good ones too.' The woman ran

her eyes over them approvingly. 'What were you doing with the maid?'

'Nothing as yet,' the boy said.

'And nothing to follow,' the woman said sharply. 'Horses are one thing, the forcing of maids another. You, girl, get down from the saddle, for you've a long way to walk home, I daresay.'

'I'm riding home,' Purity said defiantly. 'These are my father's horses and I'll not let you take them.'

'You've spirit!' the woman exclaimed. 'What's your name?'

'That's not your business either,' Purity said. Her heart was hammering but she met the other's gaze with her head high.

'No matter, I can read your history in your hand.'

The woman reached across and grabbed Purity's wrist, holding it tightly and staring down at the small ungloved palm.

'You're young and careless in many ways,' she said, 'and you've an independent nature.'

147

'You could have guessed that,' Purity said in scorn.

'True, but I'll tell you what I couldn't have guessed,' the woman said. 'You have a lover, my pretty one, but he's secret to yourself and when he goes you'll have to hide your heartache. You have a treasure too and that's another secret to yourself. And — ' She stopped, frowning down into Purity's hand.

'Is there something more?' Purity asked, fascinated despite herself by the curious intensity of the woman's gaze.

'Go your ways in peace,' the woman said at last. 'Take your horses and ride without hurt. We'll not trouble you again.'

Dropping Purity's hand she moved her own beast aside and raised her arm in a curious commanding gesture. The men surrounding her dropped back, their own faces submissive.

Purity jerked at the rein and urged her mount onward, pulling the other horse behind her. Now that the incident was over she felt weak and chilled, but when she paused to wipe the sweat trickling down her face and to glance back, fearful of the danger just passed, the moors were apparently deserted again.

She rode on more thoughtfully, recalling the woman's face and the tight grip of her fingers. It made no sense that they should let her ride on.

'Purity! What in God's Name brings you out here?'

The puzzle of the gipsies behaviour flew out of her head as Luther galloped up to her, his face full of alarm.

'Father knows about you taking the money,' she said flatly.

'What money? What are you talking about?'

'Don't bother to lie.' She slid from the saddle as he dismounted and faced him accusingly. 'Father went to York to enquire into the profits you said you'd made. He found it all out, Luther. You've lied to him and kept the money for yourself.'

'How did he find it out?'

149

'Benjamin Rathbone talked to a merchant and started to make enquiries on his own behalf.'

'He'd no call to poke his nose into my affairs!' Luther began furiously.

'Father would have discovered it for himself,' Purity said wearily. 'He says there are two hundred sovereigns missing.'

'Are there? I never counted.'

'Luther, he's informed against you,' she said tremblingly. 'Benjamin was sent to the magistrates and they'll be sure to send out a constable to take you to York. I rode out to warn you, for they'll put you in prison for sure.'

'I'll not endure that,' he said. 'It's bad enough having to live at Ladymoon Manor but to rot in a cell would drive me insane.'

'Could you not give him the money back?' she asked hopefully.

'There's scarce forty guineas left,' he told her.

'Forty guineas! But how did you

spend the rest? Where did it all go?' she demanded.

'I'm not lucky in the cocks I wager on.'

'Cocks! Luther, you know how father hates cockfighting. He says 'tis cruel and barbaric sport.'

'Don't lecture me,' her brother said sulkily. 'If he had as much care for his family as he had for the welfare of fighting cocks I'd never have been brought to this pass.'

'He'll not forgive you,' Purity said unhappily.

'Tell me something I don't already know!' Luther scuffed the grass irritably. 'I'll have to leave the neighbourhood, that's all.'

'But where will you go?' she asked in distress.

'To Cornwall!' he exclaimed, his face lighting up. 'Robert Masters willed me his land, didn't he? I'll live on it, or sell it and then go for a pirate.'

'But you've never been to Cornwall!'

'I've never been to Heaven either but

I'm hoping to go there too one day.'

'It's a wild place, and nearly all the people there are Royalists they say.'

'Then I'll turn Royalist too,' he said carelessly.

'But what of Ladymoon Manor?' she asked.

'The place never interested me,' he said, 'not even when Elisha was killed and I was told I was the new heir. Heir to what? A few flocks of sheep and a house that's miles from anywhere! You may keep it for the crows as far as I'm concerned. I'll try my luck in Cornwall.'

He had certainly changed, she thought, from the serious boy who had ridden off to war. The long conflict between king and Parliament had changed all their lives. Only Sir Joshua had remained as he had always been — fair and just according to his measure but utterly unbending in his belief that he was always in the right.

She bade farewell soberly, a strange feeling of unreality invading her. Matters were moving too swiftly and she had no time in which to analyse her own emotions.

'You'll write to me?' she asked and he nodded, holding her hands tightly, but his eyes slid away and she knew that he had no real intention of doing so. With the start of his journey south Luther was as lost to her as if he were as dead as Elisha and Hope.

There was no sense in showing her grief. She smiled instead and waved her hand as he remounted and took the Otley track again. Then she climbed to her own saddle and rode north, back among the heather clad hills.

'You've taken your time,' Sir Joshua greeted her sourly as she entered the parlour.

'Jessie's mother invited me to stay for breakfast.' Unfastening her cloak she said, a trace of pleading in her tone. 'Have you thought over what you intend to do?'

'About Luther? Exactly what I said.'

'But he may have thought — '

153

'I'm not interested in what he may or may not have thought,' he interrupted harshly.

'Have the constables arrived?'

'They may not get here until tomorrow. Benjamin did mention there are fugitive Royalists in the neighbourhood. No doubt they will be chasing after them. There are still houses in Yorkshire where a king's man can find shelter.'

'But not here? They surely would not come here?' she questioned lightly.

'Fortunately my loyalty to the Parliament has never been in question,' he said stiffly.

'Luther fought in the New Model Army,' she reminded him. 'Wouldn't that count for something?'

'When he has robbed and cheated me? It makes matters worse that he should fall from his principles now.'

'Luther may not come home,' she said hesitatingly. 'He may have taken his money.'

'It's not in his room,' he informed

her. 'I searched this morning without much hope for it's my belief he carried it on him.'

'Does Aunt Hepzibah know?'

'I told her,' he said briefly. 'She wept and railed, declaring the lad had been unhappy and more nonsense of that kind. I left her to her vapourings.'

'I'd best go to her.' She had turned towards the door, but his coldly impatient tone halted her.

'Leave her to her miseries. I want you to help prepare some extra dishes lest the constables come. With Jessie at home again we'll be short-handed until the hirings arrive.'

Luther had not mentioned having engaged any servants.

'Obediah is going over to Otley later,' Sir Joshua was continuing. 'He'll ride back with Luther and any hirings my son bothered to engage. By the time they get back the constables ought to have come, and Luther will receive a different greeting from the one he expects.'

The cold face held, beneath its icy disillusionment, a certain pleasure. Sir Joshua, Purity thought, did not expect people to behave with honour and the fact that he was so frequently right afforded him a melancholy satisfaction.

She went out into the big kitchen and began to chop vegetables in readiness for a lamb stew. The house wore its usual bustling aspect, the fire crackling on the wide hearth, the two young maids scrubbing out the pantry at the back. Her father was in the larger of the two parlours, his account books piled up before him.

In early afternoon she put bread, cheese and ale on a tray and risked taking them up to Hope's room.

James Rodale unbarred the door at her nervous tapping and she slipped within the room, motioning him to bar the door again.

'I had half a mind to emerge and spy out the land for myself,' he complained.

'Hush! Keep your voice down,' she warned. 'My father is downstairs. And there are constables due from York.'

'He suspects something?' His fair brows had rushed together in alarm.

'Not about you. My brother, Luther, has been cheating him of his profits, and my father has laid a complaint against him to the magistrates in York.'

'The canting scoundrel!' he exclaimed. 'To lay information against one's own flesh and blood!'

'He did what he believes to be right,' she said stiffly, wondering why she should trouble to defend him.

'My funny Roundhead maid!' He kissed her without passion, on the tip of her nose.

Watching him as he sat down to the food Purity experienced that quiver of desire that was becoming habitual. Unshaven, his blond curls straggling to his collar, his presence still had the power to move her.

'Obediah has ridden to Otley,' she said, wrenching her mind back to practical matters. 'He'll discover Luther isn't there.'

'How do you know that?' he enquired in surprise.

'Never mind. What matters is that he'll hare back to tell my father, and by that time the constables may have arrived. There'll be comings and goings, and no privacy anywhere.'

'It's best for me to slip away now then, while your father is still below,' he commented.

It was the wiser, she knew, but there was a little pain at her heart.

'You must be anxious to be gone,' she said, smiling to hide it.

'Anxious to be gone from this house, but not from you.'

'Is that truth and not just politeness?' she ventured.

'As true as the fact that one day the king will come into his own again and that I also will return,' he assured her.

She drew a long quivering breath of relief. To love was one thing, but to know that love was returned was another infinitely more important fact.

'You would not consider taking me with you, I suppose?' she said.

Something that might have been alarm flashed into his face, but his voice was gently regretful.

'My dear, how could we hope to take ship together? Your father would send after you and have you arrested, just as he is dealing with your brother.'

'I would be a danger to you then?'

'And in danger yourself,' he pointed out.

'I'd not mind that,' she said, 'but I would never draw capture upon you. It is only that the years pass so slowly and it gets lonely here.'

'I shall think of you,' he said, 'in your grey gown with the white coif hiding your hair and your eyes so sweet and troubled.'

It was not how she wanted to be remembered. She wanted his mind to hold an image of her naked and sweet-smelling in the darkness with her dark hair mingling with his own light locks. But there was no time.

159

'My aunt is in her room,' she said, 'and the maids and grooms out back. You can go down the hidden stairs in my father's room and through the garden down to the river. Your horse is still there, I trust.'

'What of your father?' He had risen and was putting on his jacket, reaching for cloak and hat.

'Give me one moment,' she said, her thoughts racing, 'to go into my father. He's in the parlour, but I'll keep him in conversation while you leave.'

'Clever little Roundhead!' he exclaimed. 'I am indebted to you twice over.'

'And I to you,' she said shyly.

'And I will come back,' he assured her, 'to find out if you've forgotten me or not.'

'You'd lose your wager,' she said breathlessly, and put her arms about him in a last, fervent embrace, willing with all her soul that he would remember her and keep his promise to return.

Without looking back into the room

she let herself out into the corridor again, paused to straighten her coif and compress the desire from her lips, and walked steadily down to the parlour.

Her heart gave an uncomfortable lurch as she reached the foot of the main stairs for Sir Joshua stood on the threshold of the large panelled apartment.

'Are the constables come?' she asked.

He shook his head.

'I was going in search of you. Obediah is returned with news of Luther.'

'Oh?' she followed him into the parlour.

'Luther is not in Otley,' Sir Joshua said tightly. 'Obediah made enquiries, but your precious brother had not even tried to hire any labour. He'd spent the entire day at an abominable cockfight.'

He nodded his head towards the steward who sat in a corner of the pleasantly furnished chamber. Obediah bore the same expression of satisfied melancholy as his master.

'It's true, Mistress Purity,' he confirmed. 'Master Luther's gone, last seen riding south.'

'And I'll not waste more money in chasing after him,' Sir Joshua said. 'Obediah and I are riding back to York to withdraw the complaint. In the morning I'll see my lawyer.'

'Oh?' She looked at him blankly, thinking, 'One more night to seal the joy that was begun.'

'If we meet with the constables on the road we can forestall their arrival.' Sir Joshua broke off, frowning at her. 'Don't you want to know why I'm going to see my lawyer?'

'I thought it was none of my business.'

'Now he'll be skirting the hedge in readiness for the descent to the river-bank. If I catch him he can stay hidden until father and Obediah are on their way to York and then we can have one more night together.'

'At least I have one dutiful, obedient

child,' Sir Joshua said. 'Two, for Mercy gives me no trouble. But she is comfortably settled with a husband, while you have little expectation of one. Indeed your aunt and I could not spare you at this juncture.'

'Yes, father,' she said docilely.

'Perhaps he caught his foot in a trailing creeper and stoops now to disentangle it.'

'I intend to change my Will,' he said. 'Luther is no longer any son of mine. His name will never be spoken again. When I am gone Ladymoon Manor, and all it contains, and half my money will belong to you. The rest of my money I shall leave to your sister, for I was ever a fair minded man.'

'Yes, father.' Her ears were strained to catch the distant sound of galloping hoofs.

'Go and get us something to eat before we ride.' He spoke brusquely, a little disappointed at her lack of response.

Released, she sped across the hall,

through the smaller parlour, past the kitchen door into the garden. Heedless of any who might be watching from the windows, she ran across the lawn, helter-skeltering down the slope beyond.

The tethered horse was gone and the river ran quiet. Bitter disappointment stung her eyes. She had not known until that instant how greatly she had hoped for delay. Now the years stretched ahead, full of waiting.

'But he will come back,' she said defiantly to the empty landscape. 'When the king comes into his own again.'

Part Two

1660

6

The king had returned from exile, called back by popular demand. For more than a month the decorated streets of the capital had echoed to the chime of bells and the forbidden maypoles set up in every square. The Black Boy had come into his own again and everyone was a Royalist.

Purity had felt such a lifting of the heart at the news that, for an instant, the slow years of waiting were as if they had never been, and she was twenty again. The mirror aided that illusion for her skin was still unlined, her teeth sound, her figure supple. She could have passed for several years younger than her actual age.

'He will come back now,' she said to the mirror. 'He will ride north to meet me.'

That he might not have survived

the intervening years never entered her head. Had anything terrible happened to him she was quite sure she would have known it in the deepest part of herself. But what she possessed was an inner certainty that all was well with him and that he had returned.

At Ladymoon Manor the rejoicings were modest. Had her father still been alive there would have been no rejoicings at all, but Sir Joshua had died the previous winter of a chill brought on by riding out in the snow to look for some sheep that one of the shepherds had reported missing. Since Obediah's death Sir Joshua had not engaged another steward but looked after all his affairs himself, trusting nobody.

He had kept his word, leaving the manor and its contents to his youngest child and dividing his wealth equally between her and Mercy. Of Luther there had been no word. He had vanished as completely as if the earth had swallowed him, and his name was never mentioned.

Purity had gone to York for the funeral and the reading of the Will. Afterwards as they sat in the small, bright parlour of Mercy's house, her sister had said:

'You're a rich woman now. What will you do?'

'Go back to Ladymoon Manor,' Purity said. 'Aunt Hepzibah needs almost constant care. She's very frail since her last attack.'

'But you can't spend the rest of your life nursing a sick woman,' Mercy objected.

'You should take a husband,' Benjamin said. 'It is quite scandalous that you should be still unwed. Indeed I've often wondered why your father never insisted upon your marrying before.'

'He found me too useful at home,' Purity said dryly, 'and in the matter of marriage he and I were of one accord. I am quite content with Aunt Hepzibah as companion.'

'But it is natural for a woman to have

a husband and a family,' he argued.

'You have no children,' she said irritably and bit her lip, regretting the hurt she must have caused her sister.

Mercy, however, laughed softly. 'As to that, she confided, 'we are in high hope, for I am past three months gone and carry this one secure with no hint of miscarriage!'

'After so many years? Did father know?'

'We were keeping it as a surprise,' Mercy said. 'This one will live and thrive. I'm certain of it.'

'Then I'm very happy for you,' Purity said. 'You ought to have a child. There are some women made to be mothers.'

'All women should have babes and husbands.' Benjamin returned to the attack.

'But not in that order, I trust!' she laughed.

'A rich women can easily become the prey of a fortune hunter,' he said.

'If any arrive at Ladymoon Manor,'

she said lightly, 'I'll send them to you, my dear brother-in-law! You will take care of yourself, sister?'

'I shall cosset myself,' Mercy assured her. 'You'll ride over often?'

'As often as I can. With Aunt Hepzibah so frail I cannot leave her often.'

'At least promise you'll be here for the baptism,' Mercy begged.

'You have my word on it,' Purity said gravely.

But there had been no baptism. Less than a week after her hopeful words Mercy had lost her expected child and herself died of the fever that followed.

'And out of the five of us, I am the only one left,' Purity thought.

It was a sobering reflection that she, out of them all, had survived. There was, of course, the possibility that Luther was still alive, but she felt no bond stretching between herself and her brother. On the rare occasions she thought of him she sent out a brief prayer for his safety and well-being, but as mistress of Ladymoon Manor her time was fully occupied.

The notion of riding out to inspect the flocks and enquire after missing sheep or of joining in the hustle-bustle of the York markets did not appeal to her. Instead she invited Jessie's husband, Eben Rowe, to act as steward.

'I leave the business of buying and selling, hiring and shearing entirely to you,' she informed the astonished shepherd. 'Jessie tells me that you can read and write.'

'I taught myself,' he said proudly.

'Then you will be able to keep accounts of profit and loss, and render them to me every three months?'

'Yes, Mistress Makin. I'm quick at figuring and good at driving a bargain,' he assured her.

'The profits for the first six months are yours,' Purity said. 'I cannot have my steward living three miles off, but Jessie likes her own fireside. So you'd do well to build yourself a new house at about half a mile's distance.'

It had given her a pleasant feeling of power to display such generosity. And in the months since she had often ridden out to watch the walls rising solidly to the roof.

In comparison Ladymoon Manor had seemed larger and lonelier than it had ever been. It was not that she missed her father's company but his querulous demands had given a shape to her days. Now she was free to rise when she chose and to eat her dinner when she pleased. She filled in the hours with housekeeping, dismissing all the servants save two young maids and a groom, and sometimes, in the midst of cleaning an already shining piece of silverware, she would catch herself weeping a little for no reason her mind could discover.

But the king had returned and it meant that James Rodale would be coming north.

'One day soon,' she said aloud, cupping her breasts in her hands as she stared at her reflection. It was a pity that her complexion was so sallow but at least she was never plagued by freckles or spots, and she was delicately formed with long lashes making crescents of shadow above her high cheekbones and full red mouth. Her hair was drawn back as usual under her coif and she wore the gown of black silk that signified her mourning.

Recently she had left off her weeds in the privacy of her own home and ventured into lighter colours, but this afternoon Benjamin was calling, so she retained the black silk. Looking at herself critically she wondered if a touch of rouge would enhance her skin, but Benjamin would be sure to notice and think her lacking in respect to Mercy's memory.

It was too warm for a fire but she had arranged leaves and flowers in the hearth. Now she looked at them doubtfully, wondering if Benjamin would consider them too frivolous. It was too late to do anything about it anyway. Her sharp ears had caught the sound of hoofbeats and a moment later her brother-in-law tapped at the door.

'Greetings. Let me take your things.' She accepted a dutiful kiss and laid his cloak and hat over a chair. 'You'll have wine and cake?'

'A drop of one and a morsel of the other. The ride has overheated me.' He took the seat she indicated and mopped his brow.

It was typical of him, she thought, to have ignored the new fashion for gaiety and to have retained his sober garments. His jacket and breeches were of as sad a brown as if Parliament still ruled, and his thinning hair was uncurled.

'Is Aunt Hepizibah well?' he enquired formally.

'Resting and begs you to excuse her. She had a bad night. Was your journey pleasant?'

'Well enough. My servant did arrive to warn you of my coming?'

'Yes, indeed. He's in the kitchen, sweet-talking my maids.'

'You allow your servants too much latitude,' he frowned. 'I passed the house that Eben Rowe is building for himself. Do you realise it will have three bedrooms?'

'I have seven,' she said lightly, 'not counting the loft chamber.'

'Your own position is slightly different,' he told her.

'I don't have six children like Eben and Jessie,' she agreed.

'That is why I'm here,' he said gravely.

'To lecture me on my treatment of my servants?'

'To urge upon you the necessity of having children,' he said.

'You've come matchmaking.' She gave a vexed little laugh.

'You ought to marry,' he said solemnly. 'The life you lead is an unnatural one for a female. I've often thought so.'

'You've often said so too,' she

remarked gloomily. 'I wish you'd leave off.'

'I am not here to extol the advantages of matrimony, for we have covered that ground before,' Benjamin said. 'You have never given me the impression that you are against the institution of marriage, merely that you have not yet found a husband to your liking.'

'Exactly that, so let us drop the subject.' She poured more wine and resumed her seat.

'There is one prospective husband whom we have not considered,' he persisted. 'I am conscious that you have some idea of what I mean.'

'I've not the faintest idea,' she said in surprise. 'I was under the impression you'd dangled every bachelor in Yorkshire under my nose. Don't tell me you've found one hiding in the Minster!'

'I was referring to myself,' he said.

'You.' She gaped at him.

'It is perhaps a little soon to speak for Mercy died only six months ago,'

Benjamin said, 'but I am past forty and time is not on my side. Neither, if I may say so without offence, is it on yours. You will be thirty next year.'

'I know how old I am!' she said on a note of rising temper.

'But still young enough to bear children,' he said. 'Your poor sister, for reasons the physician could never understand, was unable to carry a baby to its full term. I cast no reproach on her for that. In every other respect she was an excellent wife, and her death was a great grief to me. But I confess I am anxious for heirs and unless you marry there is nobody to inherit Ladymoon Manor when you die.'

'And you rather fancied living here yourself, didn't you? Has it slipped your mind that you were the one who warned me against fortune hunters?'

'I am very comfortably placed in my own right,' he said. 'My own silversmith's flourishes.'

'And when my sister died the share

of our father's money that she inherited passed to you.'

'A wife's property belongs to her husband.'

'But not his sister-in-law's,' she flashed. 'I'll see you a long way before you get your hands on that!'

'You're not serious, of course.'

'I was never more serious,' she said bluntly. 'I'd not wed you, Master Rathbone, if I had nothing in the world save the clothes I stood up in. But you'd not want me then, would you? You don't really want me now, do you? Not me, myself! But you crave the manor and the rest of the money my father left, and you think how fortunate it is that I'm still young enough to breed.'

'I never knew you in such a temper!' he exclaimed.

'Then you never knew me at all!' she retorted. 'I'm not like poor Hope or like Mercy. Mercy took second best and was grateful for it, but in my eyes you're not even second-best!

You're the last person I'd think of marrying!'

'I shall give you time to consider.' He rose, donning his cloak as if it were his wounded dignity. 'I'll call upon you again.'

'Don't trouble yourself, for I won't receive you,' she interrupted. 'Now you'd best whistle up your servant and ride homeward. I'll hear no more of bridegrooms!'

She slammed the door behind her without waiting for him to leave. For a moment she stood, hands clenched. Then she ran up to her aunt's room.

Aunt Hepzibah was in her tiny sitting room. Purity had hoped that Sir Joshua's death might have improved her spirits but the long years had left their mark, and Aunt Hepzibah was still in awe of the rules that had governed her life.

She looked up fearfully as her niece burst in, saying timidly, 'I hope you told Benjamin that I would have come down to greet him if I'd felt better?

Joshua was always very insistent upon good manners.'

'Don't fret yourself,' Purity said. 'We'll neither of us need to be entertaining Master Rathbone again.'

'Why, my dear, whatever do you mean?' Aunt Hepzibah said.

'Only that my kind, respectful brother-in-law offered to marry me!' Purity said.

'And from your expression I take it that you refused him.' Aunt Hepzibah cocked her head to one side and asked with unexpected shrewdness. 'Was that because you didn't like him or because you like somebody else better?'

'He behaved as if he were doing me a favour,' Purity said indignantly. 'He as good as told me that he was willing to marry me in order that he could take over the rest of my father's fortune and beget heirs upon me. He was ready to wager that I was more fertile than my sister.'

'So you sent him away.'

'And will not admit him to friendship

again until he gives up this foolish notion of marriage.'

'I have little experience of gentlemen,' Aunt Hepzibah said, 'but I cannot imagine he will give up until you are no longer available as a bride.'

'So I am to marry to keep unwanted suitors away?' Purity sat down abruptly, wondering whether to laugh or cry.

'Forgive me,' Aunt Hepzibah said, blinking nervously, 'but I have often felt these past years that you were — thinking of someone. It was not my place to intrude by asking questions.'

'There is a gentleman,' Purity said slowly. 'He's older than I am, but it never seemed like that.'

'And where did you meet?' Aunt Hepzibah asked.

'Twice in fifteen years,' Purity said wistfully. 'And each time to be held secretly and treasured. Does that sound very foolish?'

'Perhaps those who never love are even more foolish,' Aunt Hepzibah said softly. 'I take it that you could not introduce the gentleman to your father?'

'He is a King's man,' Purity said.

'Then you must tell me no more about him,' her aunt said, 'for your father brought me up to despise the Royalists, and I'm too old to change now. I take it that he's not here, in the neighbourhood, I mean.'

'He'll be in London with the Court,' Purity said.

'Then why are you up here?' her aunt demanded. 'Will he not send for you?'

'I've been waiting for him,' Purity said in a low voice. 'But he's been gone for such a long time. I've not heard from him. He may think I've forgotten him.'

'But you remembered.'

'I'd as soon forget myself,' she exclaimed. 'Twice I've met him and for all time I'm bound. There is something in me that cannot be tamed, Aunt Hepzibah, I cannot explain it.'

She paused for her aunt was hesitating

at the beginning of a sentence she was evidently framing in her mind.

'My dear — I'm not certain if I ought to tell you this.'

'Tell me what, aunt?'

'Your mother, poor Yoni — I've never talked to you about her very much. It's not that I didn't care for her, my dear. I cared for her very much, and I grieved deeply when she died.'

'My father never mentioned her either,' Purity said, 'but you need not try to tell me it was because of grief. I'm certain he never loved her.'

'It was not a happy marriage,' Aunt Hepzibah said reluctantly. 'Not many marriages are happy, I think. Oh, they got along well enough. There were no open quarrels, only a coldness that spread itself around them and covered the whole house. I was never certain why she agreed to marry him, but her father was ailing and Yoni was always a dutiful daughter. It was not until after the wedding that we discovered — '

'Discovered what?' Purity asked sharply.

'Yoni was — it seems so wrong to tell you, even though she said I must use my own judgement in the matter.'

'My mother wished you to tell me something?'

'When she was dying, after you were born,' Aunt Hepzibah said, 'I nursed her. She knew she hadn't long to live, but she was very brave. She was anxious about you, anxious because she feared life would be harsh for you with no mother. I fear my brother had little affection in his nature.'

'What was it she wished you to tell me about?' Purity asked.

'When we came up into Yorkshire,' Aunt Hepzibah said, 'and she agreed to marry Joshua we knew nothing of her save that she was of good family. It was not until after the wedding that we learned the truth. She flung it at us in temper.'

It was no use to hurry her, else she would become flustered and lose the thread of her discourse. Gritting her teeth, Purity said, 'What did she tell you, aunt?'

'That she was not born to the parents who reared her,' Aunt Hepzibah said in distress. 'There is no blame attached to anybody at all in such a matter. There are women who cannot have babes. Poor Mercy was one such. And if they take another woman's child, rearing it as their own, why there's great merit in that.'

'Who was my mother?' Purity asked. 'Who were her real parents?'

'She was a foundling,' her aunt said. 'A gypsy child, abandoned on a doorstep one cold winter's night in York.'

'A gypsy!' Into Purity's mind had flashed that scene from nine years before when she had ridden to warn Luther and been accosted by the gypsies.

'It sounds very shocking, I know.' Aunt Hepzibah patted her arm comfortingly. 'But Yoni was only part gypsy, I believe,

186

for she was blonde and blue eyed, and never could be taken for Romany unless anyone knew.'

'But I am dark,' Purity said. 'Dark as any gypsy.'

'And the wildness in you — I've seen it, though you hold it in check — I believe that comes from your mother's people too.'

'So she was gypsy,' Purity mused. 'Was she abandoned?'

'More likely lost or strayed,' said Aunt Hepzibah. 'I believe Romanies take good care of their young as a rule. But that winter was a harsh one, and she may have been sent out to beg. She was about five years old when she was found.'

'Poor Yoni!' Purity exclaimed.

'You mustn't dwell upon it too sadly,' counselled Aunt Hepzibah. 'She had a very happy childhood in York. Her nature was gay and loving.'

'But not to her husband.'

'Poor Joshua could neither inspire love nor return it,' said Aunt Hepzibah.

'You have nothing of him in you, save a little of his determination perhaps. But your loving comes from your dear mother.'

'And I must be true to myself,' Purity said. 'You were right to tell me. I'm not shocked or ashamed, you know.'

'I was so very fond of her,' the older woman said. 'She deserved a kinder husband. Her death was more a grief to me than to her, for in the end she seemed almost happy. Her mind had wandered to a kind of fairy-tale land, I think, for she talked of golden goblets and a woman who lived in the moon.'

'Golden goblets? Are you sure? What did she say?'

'It was just rambling, dear. Many ramble in their minds at the point of death.'

'But what exactly did she say?' Purity insisted.

'Something about a golden goblet older than the first house that stood there. She kept repeating over and over 'The woman dwells in the moon'. It made no sense, of course. And then she died.'

So Sir Joshua had not known about the cup, nor hidden it under the floor of the prayer chamber. It had been Yoni who had, somehow or other, discovered it and kept the secret of its hiding place.

'If I decided to pay a visit to London,' Purity said abruptly, 'would you be content to stay here with Jessie to take care of you? I'd not be gone for longer than a month.'

'You're going to seek your lover.' Aunt Hepzibah said.

'Would that be so very wrong?' Purity asked. 'Would it displease you very much?'

The other was silent for a few moments, and when she spoke her voice was wistful.

'I told you once that I had been in love and was parted from him. If I had possessed more courage I might have gone to seek him, refused to move north with my brother. If Yoni had been a little braver she might have refused to tie herself to a loveless marriage. We cannot make rules for other people.'

'But if you were me, what would you do?'

'I'd not betray my own heart,' said Aunt Hepzibah.

Purity bent and hugged her, feeling with a little pang the too-sharp bones under the black gown. Her aunt was growing daily weaker, her breathing shorter, her cheeks more vividly red.

'If I am to travel to London,' Purity thought, 'it'll be best for me to start soon, or she'll be too sick for me to risk leaving her with Jessie.'

Benjamin Rathbone had long since ridden away, evidently displaying his ill-humour, for when she walked into the kitchen Janet and Sally broke off an animated conversation and made a great bustle at the sink.

'I'm going to ride over to the Rowe

house,' she told them. 'Tell Nat to saddle the bay, and be sure to answer my aunt's bell if she rings it.'

'Master Rathbone didn't have time to stay over for supper then?' Janet enquired innocently.

'No. No, he didn't. Are you sure that pan's scoured?'

'I can give it another do if you like, mistress,' Janet said.

'I do like. Sally, go and find Nat — and don't stand chattering to him about other folks' business.'

Both girls turned faces of shocked reproach towards her.

'Oh, mistress, we'd never shame ourselves so!' Sally cried.

'Very virtuous of you. See that you keep your resolution,' Purity said dryly.

They were good girls, she thought, prone to gossip and giggle, but honest and faithful, and romantically excited about the return of the king.

Up in her room she changed into the grey riding habit that Sir Joshua had allowed her to buy the previous summer. He had not really approved of women riding alone, but Purity had found great satisfaction in the exercise.

The habit with its high collar and tight sleeves was, like all her garments, without ornament or trimming. Her hat was decorated only with a curled white feather. She studied herself critically, wondering how she would look in a gown of jewel red or deep turquoise or flaming, flashing yellow. And surely, now that the king sat upon his throne again, ladies of fashion would wear jewels and flowers and velvet ribbons. She possessed none of those things.

'James Rodale will have to take me as I am,' she said aloud. 'I'll not strut like a peacock to tease his palate.'

Time enough after she had found him to buy jewels and fine clothes. She would travel to London in sober garments and he would see the Roundhead maid whom he had loved and left nine years before.

Picking up her crop she went briskly

down to the stables, whistling under her breath, a thing she would not have dared to do when Sir Joshua was alive.

The workmen were hurrying to roof the house before the winter snow and rain set in. She reined in her mare to admire the solid, stone structure with the spaces blank where the doors and windows would be. There were six good sized rooms, with a staircase to connect them, and they had begun to sink a well at a little distance.

'Mistress Purity!' Eben Rowe broke off the instructions he was giving to a couple of labourers and came over to her, his expression pleased but faintly apprehensive. 'There's nothing wrong, I trust? It's not the day for rendering accounts?'

'I'm travelling to London in a day or so,' Purity said, trying to sound as if it were the most natural thing in the world for her to uproot herself. 'Business matters and some private affairs. Can you and Jessie move into the manor while I'm away? I'll not be gone longer than a month, but I'll be easier in my mind about Aunt Hepzibah if there are responsible folk in charge. Sally and Janet are good girls but — '

'Feckless,' said Eben, nodding his head. 'You may rely on me, mistress. Jessie's mother will have the bairns and we'll see that all's well at the manor. 'Tis the least we could do after all your kindness to us.'

'I intend to take Janet with me as maidservant,' she explained. 'I want to hire a conveyance too and a driver. Can you arrange something?'

'I can indeed, mistress. You leave it in my hands.' He paused a second and then ventured, 'You're sure there's nothing wrong? I'd not have you troubled.'

'Everything is going to be wonderful,' she said, suddenly confident that it would be.

'I'm glad of it, mistress,' he said. 'Jessie and I were only saying the other day that if anybody deserves a little happiness in this world it's yourself, if you'll excuse the liberty.'

'Thank you, Eben.' She lifted her hand in salute and rode away.

Excitement was mounting in her. The feelings of unrest that had simmered in her for so long were bursting forth into action. She had been foolish to wait until he came. In this world one gained the prize by going to seek it.

She rode easily, her hands slack on the reins, her eyes dreaming across the purple and gold moor. But on this day she was thinking, not of the beauties of the landscape, but of the spires and streets of the distant city.

'Me to go with you to London!' Janet gasped at her in disbelief.

'To act as my lady's maid,' Purity said firmly. 'I cannot spare Sally for her cooking suits Aunt Hepzibah's digestion. But you have a clever hand with a needle, and I think you could learn how to dress hair in a fashionable manner.'

'You're going to be a lady of fashion, mistress?' Janet looked even more astounded.

'I may very well be just that,' Purity said serenely. When she had eaten her supper and settled Aunt Hepzibah for the night, she went into the prayer-chamber. Since her father's death she had confined household prayers to a blessing before supper, but the room itself still drew her.

She rolled back the carpet, slid aside the tile and lifted out the golden cup. She had lit two candles and their twin flames were reflected in the curving sides of the goblet. The silver etched face of the mysteriously smiling woman was haloed in the flickering radiance.

Older than the original Roman house that had once occupied the site of Ladymoon Manor. Her mother had babbled of it as she lay dying. Poor Yoni, ashamed of her gypsy blood, wed to a man for whom she had no affection! But she had found the cup and kept the secret of its existence until her death.

'Ladymoon,' Purity said aloud and wondered if whoever built the house had known about the cup, and named the house after the woman on the cup. Purity was not sure why the woman reminded her of the moon, unless it was that she herself had always loved that pale planet.

The moon was rising now, spreading itself across the evening sky, flaunting her ripe beauty. Purity lifted the cup higher and spoke softly.

'I swear on the moon, the eternal moon, that I will seek and find James Rodale. I love him now as I loved him nine years ago, when he taught me to be a woman and not a shivering girl. I swear on the blood of my poor mother, and the hopes I hold, and the beauty of every falling star. I'll find him and he will not have forgotten me.'

7

Never, even in York, had such a cacophony of sound assaulted her ears. On every side rose the cries of hucksters, the rattling of coach wheels, the jangling of bells that seemed to echo and re-echo from one steeple to the next.

'Lord, mistress! all the world must be here to see the king!' Janet gasped, plucking at Purity's sleeve.

'There are many here,' Purity agreed.

Her heart sank a little as she looked round at the jostling crowds. They had been only a day or two in London, but she had realised that finding James Rodale was not going to be a simple matter. The city was bursting at the seams, and it was only with great difficulty that she had succeeded in obtaining rooms at a respectable hostelry by Lincoln's Inn Fields.

The rooms were clean and comfortable and she had quelled the landlord's doubting look by paying for a month's board and lodging in advance.

'For I have a fancy to see the sights of the town, sir,' she explained.

'And there are plenty of those,' he assured her, unbending a little when he had bitten the coins to his own satisfaction. 'Cockfights and bull-baiting and the lions in the Tower and the playhouses rushing to reopen. Firework displays and public balls too at the Vauxhall Gardens, but 'tis wise for a lady to go escorted there, the crowds being rough and unmannerly.'

'I am hoping to see His Majesty,' she confided.

'You and ten thousand others,' he said genially. 'If you pay a small fee you may watch him eat his dinner at Whitehall any day of the week. But if you'll pardon me for mentioning it, Mistress Makin, fashions are much gayer since the king returned, and your own dress is somewhat plain.'

'My father died at the beginning of the year,' Purity explained. 'However I do feel something more fashionable would not be disrespectful to his memory'

'We're all Royalists now,' said the landlord wisely. 'If you're wishing to refurbish your wardrobe you couldn't do better than to consult Mistress Carstairs. She is the best dressmaker in London even if she is my late wife's cousin. I could ask her to step round if you give me the word.'

A little amused at his angling for custom on behalf of a relative, Purity agreed to give the word for Mistress Carstairs to step round.

She had proved to be a trim, round-eyed little woman who talked with shut lips as if she were forever holding a row of pins in her mouth. Her own gown was of sombre black but she rattled on without stopping about the virtues of colour.

'Ivory and peach will suit your colouring, mistress. I have a length of the daintiest flowered sarcenet in just those shades. A soft red too will look lovely with your dark hair. Skirts are narrower this season and sleeves fuller, and coifs quite out of style unless you are an old lady, which I make bold to declare you are not! There is a new mulberry shade which would be vastly becoming if it were highlighted by loops of silver ribbon. My assistants and I have been snowed under with orders since the Court returned, but seeing my cousin recommended you I'd be happy to lay all else aside in order to fulfil your request and only for the very smallest extra consideration.'

Purity had weakly consented to order an ivory and peach day gown, a mulberry and silver ball gown, and a cloak of rich red under which she could wear one of the dun-coloured dresses she had brought with her. She possessed no jewels and was not inclined to waste her money on any of the expensive trinkets displayed in the shop windows, but she bought flowers made of coloured lace and a number of fine cock's feathers to ornament her new riding hat.

Meanwhile, taking Janet with her, she ventured out into the teeming streets. Never had she known such bustle, such a to-ing and fro-ing of wooden pattens, and carriage wheels, and iron-shod hoofs on the cobbled paving stones of the intricately winding streets. Janet, her eyes popping, could not contain her astonishment at the bewigged gallants in their puffed breeches and wide trunk hose and lace smothered shirts.

'And patches, mistress. Shapes of black velvet cut out and pasted all over his face! Did you ever see anything so outlandish in your life!'

'It probably covers up pockmarks,' Purity began, but Janet, squealing, had just ducked away to escape a cascade of muddy water whipped up by a passing carriage.

London was not only crowded and colourful. It was also incredibly noisy and dirty. The streets were encrusted with filth, the buildings coated with soot from the belching chimneys; the constant clatter assaulted the ears, and within a few hours Purity had been glad of a perfumed handerchief to hold over her nose and mouth in order to protect herself from the stomach wrenching stench.

But there was beauty too. She hired two ponies and went riding in St. James's Park, feeling at home amid the rolling green slopes banked with flowers that bloomed for only a little season in the north.

She went out, also, to Chelsea Village where she and Janet ate strawberries and cream and watched prettily dressed Society ladies giggle and squeak as they inexpertly milked dainty Jersey cows and handed the beribboned mugs to their escorts.

But she had not lost sight of her reason for travelling to London. In those first two weeks there was not a morning when she didn't wake with the thought, 'Today I might see James

Rodale.' And at night a candle burning on the low sill of her chamber, she risked the evening air and sat for a long time, looking out over the huddled roofs, listening to the whistles of the boatmen along the river, wondering where James Rodale slept or if he were dancing at some reception or other.

The landlord, William Rogue whose kindly disposition belied his name, had begun to take an almost paternal interest in his guest. There was, he decided, some mystery in her background. She was evidently a gentlewoman and he surmised that she was not without wealth, but her dark eyes and hair had something foreign in their aspect and it was odd that so comely a woman should be still unwed and without escort.

'It's my belief 'tis her lover who died, not her father,' he told Mistress Carstairs, 'and the dear young lady has come to London to forget.'

'More likely to seek another lover,' Mistress Carstairs retorted. 'You'd best have a care, Will, for you've been two years a widower and I've noticed signs of restlessness in you lately.'

'Faith, but she'd have none of me,' he said, though the remark tickled his vanity. He was, after all, scarce past forty and had managed to remain fairly prosperous, even during the Protectorate, when inns and ale-houses were frowned upon by the authorities, and often shut down on slight excuse.

He did however, obtain three tickets for admission to the Palace of Whitehall and was delighted when Purity accepted his offer of escort.

'For a lady alone at Whitehall may very well be approached by some undesirable man,' he had earnestly explained.

'I look forward to it,' she said truthfully. 'It will be a fine thing to see King Charles.'

The palace itself was so enormous that she wondered aloud how His Majesty could ever possibly find his way about.

'I don't suppose he even knows how many rooms there are,' Master Rogue said, leading the way rather importantly up a wide flight of steps into yet another paved courtyard.

'Nor how many people live here, I dare say.' She looked about her at the thronging crowd.

'Most of them are sightseers with tickets like us,' he explained. 'There are clerks and Civil Servants and many seeking employment here too. A raggle taggle of Royalists, you might say, for many of them were ruined in the war and come here to claim back their lands and wealth. Not that they've much hope, for it's rumoured the king has no money either.'

And that, Purity decided as they presented their tickets and joined the long line of people filing into the Banqueting Hall, was surely nonsense, for she had never seen such a magnificent place in her life.

Scarlet ropes made a passage around the great, domed apartment, dividing sightseers from those who occupied the gilded chairs ranged down one side of the long table. Covered by a snowy cloth it was set with gold plate, delicate crystal and painted china.

'Can you see the king, mistress?' Janet was whispering. 'The tall one with the long black curls?'

Janet was become as ardent a Royalist as anyone in the city.

'He looks very solemn,' Purity whispered back.

Privately she thought that he was ugly, his features heavy, his mouth twisted down at the corners as if everything he saw afforded him a cynical amusement. He seemed to be eating heartily, oblivious to the crowds. Oblivious too to the fact that in this room his father had been beheaded in full view of his weeping subjects — or perhaps by dining here, he hoped to wipe away the stain of the past. She paused, watching as he rose, glass in hand, and made a graceful acknowledgement to the crowd.

'The lady next to the king is Mistress Palmer,' William Rogue was saying. 'She appears everywhere with him as if she were queen.'

Purity heard herself say something in reply, but at that moment she saw neither the king nor his mistress. Her gaze was fixed upon the tall, broad shouldered man who stood within the ropes, his back half-turned as he carried on what was evidently an amusing conversation with two other gallants.

The last time she had seen him he had worn a dirty jacket and a bedraggled hat, but she was not mistaken. She could not possibly have forgotten that characteristic slouch, the curling hair, more silver now than fair, the long legs that once had pressed her down into willing surrender.

An impatient sightseer, on tiptoe behind, poked her in the back and she was moving forward again, willing James Rodale to look in her direction.

'The ceiling is very grand, Mistress Makin,' William Rogue was saying.

'The king will not allow candles to be used in here lest the smoke ruin the colours, so he has his suppers, the public ones that is, in an adjoining apartment where the decorations are not so fine.'

The ceiling might have been wattle and daub for all she cared. Eyes burning in a face from which all colour had fled she moved on, her cold hand sliding along the rope, her heart winging across the marble space between James Rodale and herself.

Surely she had not waited so long, nor travelled so far, to pass by him unseen! The king had risen and was toasting the crowd again. There was an outburst of clapping. She was pressed against the ropes by those behind who struggled for a better view.

As he turned and looked full at her she waved her hand in a desperate wave and mouthed his name under cover of the cheering. Then the crowd surged on again and she was swept through the wide doors into the gallery beyond.

'I wonder how the poor king contrives to eat a decent meal with all those folk looking on,' Janet was marvelling.

'You look very pale, Mistress Makin. Was it too crowded for you?' William Rogue was enquiring.

She looked past him and saw James Rodale hesitating a few yards beyond.

'I am a little dizzy,' she answered automatically.

'If you would like to sit down I'll go and obtain some refreshment. One can buy fruit and wine somewhere, I believe.'

'If you please.' She sat down on the marble bench behind her and nodded at Janet. 'Go with Master Rogue and help him carry everything back.'

'Are you sure you'll be all right, mistress?' Janet asked.

'Perfectly. Don't fuss, girl, but do as I bid.' There was an irritable little snap in her voice. Janet, giving her a faintly puzzled look, followed Master Rogue's thickset figure.

'Is it truly the Roundhead maid?'

His voice had not changed, though there were more lines in his face than she remembered, and a moustache hid his upper lip.

'Am I changed so greatly?' she asked, trying to smile, but finding, to her chagrin, that there were tears pricking her eyes.

'Not in yourself, but the gown is new. Was that your husband who dashed away in search of refreshment?'

'I have no husband!' she exclaimed. 'How could you imagine such a thing? Master Rogue is landlord of the inn where I'm staying.'

'Did your father bring you to London? He must have changed his opinions since I knew him!'

'My father has been dead many months,' she said. 'I am the only one of my family left now, except Aunt Hepzibah and she is sick.'

'Then you're still at Ladymoon Manor?'

'I own it,' she said with a touch of pride. 'The manor and the sheep and all that my father left. I am mistress of it all now, and so do as I please.'

'So I see. And doing as you please means coming to London to gape at the king, does it? You are a Royalist now, like everyone else in the land.'

'I am myself,' she said simply, 'and I came to London in search of you.'

'For all you knew I might have been dead!'

'Something would have told me,' she said, 'but nothing did. I knew that you had got safely away, and I knew that you would come back when the king did. I waited for you up in Yorkshire, but you didn't come.'

'My dear, I am past fifty,' he said. 'How could I have expected you to wait for my coming?'

'Did you never think of me?' she asked in a small voice.

'Often and with great yearning,' he said, 'but I was so sure you would be wed that I determined to let the past die into memory. You're so very young.'

'I'm nearly thirty,' she told him, 'not the girl you met down by the river. I told you once that I would never lie to you, nor betray you, and that promise I've kept.'

'And now you're a rich, independent woman!' He laughed, throwing back his head and took her two hands in his. 'Little Purity Makin!'

'And still true,' she said in a low voice. 'I want you to know that.'

'We cannot talk here. There are too many people. Where are you staying?'

'The Two Pigeons, at Lincoln's Inn Fields.'

'Can you slip away alone this evening?' he asked. 'We have so much to talk about. I'll have a coach waiting.'

'At about nine-o-clock? I'll be there.'

A swift kiss on the back of her hand and he had gone back into the Banqueting Hall. The crowds blocked her view and William Rogue was coming back with a basket of fruit in one hand and a mug of what was probably cider or malmsey in the other. It didn't matter. Nothing in the world mattered save the fact that James Rodale had come back, and she was certain that he still cared for her.

It was easier than she expected to slip away unobserved. Master Rogue, having taken a brief holiday from the inn, was too busy grumbling to his apprentice about the day's takings and the stains on the bar-room floor to notice her. Janet, over-excited by the day's happenings, had gone early to bed.

Wearing the new red cloak over her plain grey gown Purity went softly down the stairs, through the hall, under the swinging sign, into the darkening street. A clock somewhere was chiming nine, but a closed coach already waited a few yards away, and as she began to walk towards it, James Rodale descended the steps and caught her hands in his.

'You're very punctual, and yet I'm already impatient,' he said.

'I didn't mean to keep you waiting,' she said.

'My love, I have kept you waiting for nine years!'

'And would not have come to me in the end,' she settled herself within the cool darkness of the coach.

'Because I thought you would have, at the very least, outgrown your affection for me. Young love is a fleeting thing.'

'You did me a great injustice, sir,' she reproached. 'I have been strictly bred and would never have given myself without love.'

'I thought myself too old for you.'

'I never cared for green lads,' she said softly, and was silent again in his embrace.

'I have a room at Whitehall. Not, I fear, as splendid as the one where His Majesty dines, but an equerry must be content with what he can get,' he said, at last.

'Are you an equerry?' she enquired, impressed.

215

'It is not as grand as it sounds,' he warned. 'My duties consist of standing about most of the time making polite conversation, or running errands for His Majesty. It is not a life I enjoy.'

'But to be at Court!'

'I have spent the last nine years at some Court or other,' he said ruefully. 'Holland, France, even a brief visit to Spain. All Courts are the same in the end. One longs for the peace of the countryside, for the values of one's boyhood.'

He sounded weary and disillusioned.

'Where are we going,' she asked, her tone bright in an effort to cheer him up.

'I have taken the liberty of assuming you'll sup with me.'

'At Whitehall?'

'The only home I have,' he said, 'but my servant Jeremy, will wait upon us.'

'I ought to have worn my evening gown.'

'My sweet Roundhead, did you imagine I asked you to supper for the sake of your wardrobe?' he retorted. 'You would be welcome in your shift!'

'And that would cause a very great scandal.'

'Not at this Court. His Majesty has a secret stair behind his own bedchamber which leads down to the water's edge where a boat is moored ready to take the king wherever he chooses. Mistress Palmer does not satisfy all the royal appetites.'

She giggled, a delicious sense of adventure stealing through her bones. If her father had ever dreamed that his youngest daughter would, one day, be on her way to sup, unchaperoned, with the king's equerry. Surely, if he knew it now, he was bombarding his fierce and unyielding god with complaints!

The coach stopped and they alighted at a staircase. Above them a lounging sentry snapped to attention and, at a nod from James Rodale, lowered his sword.

Within the oaken doors a wide corridor led to a shorter flight of steps. They passed through a second set of doors and were in a candlelit antechamber where a youngish man, in the livery of a servant, waited respectfully.

'Good evening, Jeremy.' James divested himself of hat and cloak and unbuckled his short sword. 'I hope the supper is not spoiled?'

'Hot from the kitchen, sir, and if I may make so bold, as sweet a supper as you'd hope to eat anywhere in London!'

'Jeremy bullies the cooks if they are male and seduces them if they are female,' James told her, leading the way into the apartment beyond.

It was, she supposed, a bedchamber, for a wide bed occupied an alcove in one wall, but the rest of the room was furnished as a parlour with hangings of a deep apricot brocade and a small table laid with an assortment of dishes.

'I trust you like oysters,' James said, lifting her cloak from her shoulders. 'And the lamb in coriander is a delicate dish. The King himself is very partial to it, but Jamie has a fancy for more highly spiced foods.'

'Jamie?'

'The king's brother, the Duke of York. He is known as Jamie to those whom he honours with his friendship.'

'And this is a beautiful room,' she said.

'Your presence enhances it. Shall we talk while we eat?' He was drawing out a chair for her, and Jeremy was coming in with a chafing dish.

'There is little for me to tell,' she said. 'My father died last winter.'

'And left you his property, you said. But what of his other children?'

'My brother Elisha was killed long ago and Luther — Luther offended my father very greatly and was disowned.'

'Where is he now?' He helped her to cream sauce.

'Dead, I suppose. He went away into Cornwall and we never heard from him again. And both my sisters are dead too.'

'So there is only you.'

'And Aunt Hepzibah,' she nodded. 'But she grows weaker day by day. I was anxious about leaving her, but I had to come.'

'So you're a woman of property!' He leaned back, raising his glass to her.

'I suppose I am.' She laughed. 'But I leave my affairs in the hands of my steward, Eben Rowe. He sees to the buying and selling of the sheep and to the profits from the wool.'

'I hope he's honest.'

'As honest as the day,' she assured him. 'He is building a house for himself and his family about a mile from the manor.'

'But surely you and your aunt are not alone in that great house!' he exclaimed.

'We have two maids — Janet is with me in London now — and a cook, and a couple of grooms — ' She broke off, laughing again. 'But how dull my domestic arrangements must sound to a man who spends his life at Court!'

'Anything you do is fascinating to me,' he said earnestly. 'I couldn't begin to tell you how often, when I was away on the Continent, my mind turned to you. I wondered what you were doing, what you were thinking about. You were so very clear in my mind.'

'As you were.' She raised her own glass to him.

'I was a fool,' he said sombrely, 'not to have travelled up to Yorkshire as soon as I returned. But I thought it would be a useless journey. And though I wished you every happiness and would not have grudged you a moment's joy I don't believe I could have borne it, to see you with another man.'

'There has been nobody,' she said.

'I wish I could give you the same assurance,' he said in a low voice. 'But nine years is a long time and men have needs that must be satisfied.'

'I have asked you nothing,' Purity said quickly.

'One thing I can promise you,' he

continued, 'is that no other woman except you ever held my heart for more than a few minutes. And with you — am I wrong in believing that it is not yet too late?'

'No. You're not wrong,' she said.

'Then I have something for you.' He rose from the table and went over to a tallboy against the wall. Having extracted a paper from a drawer he came back, handing it to her with something of a flourish.

'What is it?' she asked in bewilderment, looking at the slanting writing, the illuminated crest at the foot of the page.

'A marriage licence,' he said, 'giving James Rodale and Purity Makin the right to wed within forty-eight hours. I took the liberty of applying for it this afternoon. It bears the royal cipher as you see.'

'Yes, I do. Does that mean the king had to grant permission for you to wed?'

'I am not so important,' James

said, returning to his seat. 'But as an equerry I do have certain duties to fulfil. Fortunately His Majesty was in excellent humour this afternoon, and agreed that, in future, my duties at Court might be curtailed so that most of my time could be spent up north.'

She was motionless, her cooling supper forgotten, her eyes shining.

'Did I do wrong?' he asked her. 'Was I mistaken in believing that you would be willing to marry me at once?'

'No. Oh, no! I will wed you, happily at any time,' she said. 'But within forty-eight hours? I have no wedding-gown, no witnesses.'

'So after nine years you propose to start sewing your wedding dress! Purity, you are a typical female!' he exclaimed in delight. 'You look perfect as you are. Doesn't she look perfect?'

He appealed to the servant who had entered with another course on a silver tray.

'Indeed she does, Master Rodale,' Jeremy said promptly.

'You mean that you wish us to be married at once?' she faltered.

'We can get hold of a minister, can we not? James asked his servant.

'The Reverend Peabody might be persuaded to oblige, if I were to let him know His Majesty has given leave.'

'The Duke of Abermarle's Chaplain? Do you think he would agree?'

'He's in residence at the Palace. I could ask him for you,' Jeremy offered. 'They do say he's a very amiable gentleman, with a strong romantical streak.'

'We shall need two witnesses,' James said. 'Will you stand for us, Jeremy?'

'Gladly, sir. And Sergeant Muskin would stand too, I believe, for he's on equerry guard tonight.'

'See to it,' James said.

'It's all happening so quickly,' Purity said weakly.

'Are you regretting your answer already?' he asked.

'Forgive me, for after so long an absence I have no right to rush you into any scheme. But after so long an absence, have I not also the right to be just a little impatient?'

'I regret nothing,' she said swiftly. 'It is only that when a dream suddenly comes true it makes one a trifle dizzy.'

'Or you have drunk a little too much wine,' he teased. 'Eat a little of this meringue. It is a pity to let the rest of our supper go to waste.'

'Now I believe that you're a Yorkshireman born,' she teased in return, 'for only a Yorkist would bother about wasting a supper!'

'Dear Roundhead!' He gave her a gentle look. 'After waiting so long you should have had a silver gown and a bridesmaid and a cake of icing sugar! Do you want me to send after Jeremy and tell him we have decided upon delay?'

'We'll wait no longer,' Purity said firmly. 'Why, Aunt Hepzibah will be astonished to meet you.'

'But I have already made her acquaintance,' he reminded her. 'Long ago, when your mother was betrothed to Sir Joshua, I met his sister briefly then. She was a meek, mousy creature if I recall all right. I've no doubt she'll have forgotten me. Indeed, if she does remember, she may disapprove. I am so very much older than you are.'

'Aunt Hepzibah approves of everything I do,' Purity said serenely. 'She will be happy to have a master at Ladymoon Manor again.'

'The house and the sheep are your concern,' he said quickly. 'I'll not interfere.'

'And I'll not interfere with your duties at Court,' she promised. 'Will they take you often away from me?'

'As seldom as I can contrive it. That sounds like Jeremy now! I'd best go and smooth down the Reverend Peabody. He may be the most amiable cleric in the land but nobody enjoys being hauled out of a warm bed to conduct a wedding. Give me a few moments, my love.'

He dropped a kiss on the end of her

nose and went out, closing the double doors behind him.

The supper was congealing on the plates, and the meringue was beginning to sink down into itself. She pushed the dishes aside and sipped at the rest of her wine.

'Mistress Purity Rodale,' she said aloud and laughed, excitement gripping her again.

It was too fantastic, she thought, for her to grasp it all at once. The long quiet years of lonely waiting had drawn to a close, and her adventure had borne the fruit of all her youthful desires. 'Mistress Purity Rodale,' she said again and, raising her glass, solemnly toasted the empty room.

8

In after years, when she had the benefit of hindsight, Purity decided that her unhappiness had begun with their return to Ladymoon Manor. Her hurried marriage had held for her all the ingredients of high romance, and the journey north had been a pleasant one. They had started for home within the day, waved off by a regretful William Rogue who privately considered she had made a grave mistake in wedding somebody other than himself. Janet, bouncing on the seat of the hired coach, was full of excitement for the servants had privately agreed that their mistress was unlikely to marry, and now here she was with a handsome husband. To be sure he was past middle age, but his manners were charming, and he treated Mistress Makin as if he feared the wind would blow on her.

They arrived at Ladymoon Manor to drawn blinds and black crepe tied upon the knocker. Jessie, her sleeves rolled up and her apron awry, was cleaning the step. Her eyes welled with tears as she came to greet them.

'You must have left before the message arrived in London, mistress,' she said. 'The carter from Otley promised to make speed but he must have passed you somewhere on the road, not knowing it was you.'

'Is it Aunt Hepzibah?'

Jessie nodded, her lip quivering. 'It was only a slight attack, mistress. She's had many such before, but Eben fetched the physician from York, just to be on the safe side. She had another attack just after he arrived and there was no remedy. We did everything we could.'

'I'm sure you did, Jessie.' She patted the woman's shoulder consolingly.

'Jessie, Mistress Purity is wed,' Janet burst out, unable to contain her news a moment longer.

'Wed? Is that really so, Mistress Purity?' Eben, coming round the corner in time to hear the words, gave her a look of unflattering surprise.

'This is my husband, Master James Rodale,' she said. 'James, Eben Rowe is my steward, and his wife, Jessie, is more friend than servant.'

'I've heard tell of you both.' James bowed, his smile friendly but restrained. 'I am only too sorry that our homecoming should be marred by sad news.'

'First Sir Joshua, then Mistress Mercy, now Mistress Hepzibah. Death always comes in threes,' Jessie said sadly.

'Is she in her room?' Purity asked.

'Sally and I laid her out as comely as you'd wish,' Jessie said.

'I'll go up to her. Will you look after Master Rodale, and see to the coachman? He'll need a bed for the night before he starts back.'

'Do you want my company?' James asked.

'Later, I'll go up alone first.' She stepped within, lifting her skirts free of the wet floor, paused to exchange a word with Sally who was at the kitchen door, and went upstairs.

Aunt Hepzibah was laid in the tiny room she had used as a sitting-room for more than thirty years.

The room itself was clean and bare, the shutters closed, her sewing folded neatly on a chair. It was still unfinished and on Aunt Hepzibah's face was a faint astonishment as if Death had taken her by surprise.

But there was nothing in the room to awaken more than a gentle regret. Hepzibah Makin had crept out of the world as shyly as she had occupied it.

Purity took a long look at the white face and the neatly coiled bands of greying hair and went out again, closing the door softly as if she were closing the last page of a favourite book.

In the passage Eben met her, a trunk under his arm, a puzzled expression in his face.

'Master Rodale told me to put his things in Mistress Hope's old room,' he said. 'Is that in order, Mistress?'

'Whatever my husband says.' She nodded at him briskly and went down into the parlour where James was eating a meal laid out on the small table. He rose at once as she came in, his voice and glance tender.

'This is a sad welcome for you, my love.'

'Aunt Hepzibah would have been so pleased for me,' she said simply.

'You were fond of her.'

'Very fond. She was the only mother I remember and she never had much of a life. All those years with my father to dominate her, and she was in bad health for so long. I'll have to take her to York. All my family are buried there.'

'Sit down and eat something first,' he urged, 'before you rush about making arrangements. I've no doubt Eben Rowe will be seeing to matters. He strikes me as efficient.'

'Very much so.' She helped herself to a leg of chicken. 'He was putting your luggage upstairs.'

'I told him to do so.'

'In Hope's old room. I had intended to use the master bedroom — '

'Too gloomy,' he said firmly. 'I could not sleep there without dreaming of your father.'

'But for both of us — we could redecorate, refurnish.'

'My dear Roundhead.' He was looking at her in affectionate amusement. 'In fashionable circles husband and wife do not occupy the same rooms!'

'Do they not?' she enquired in surprise.

'Adjoining rooms keep alive that aura of mystery that should stretch between lover and lover.'

'Between lover and lover there should be no distance,' she said in a small voice.

'Sweetheart, you're a delightful little rustic!' he exclaimed. 'But you cannot pretend you would enjoy hearing me snore night after night, or wake in the dawn to find me bleary-eyed and unshaven. As it is, if you need me, I am only in the next room. And we will spend most hours of the night together, unless you grow tired of me quickly.'

'I shall never do that,' she said warmly, but there was a trace of hurt in her tone, for his own face darkened.

'You are not going to turn into one of those wives who will not permit their husbands a moment's privacy, are you?' he asked lightly.

'No, of course not!'

'You will have to give me time to become accustomed to marriage,' he said, 'for when a man is past fifty it's hard for him to settle.'

'Adjoining rooms will do very well,' she said stiffly.

'In that way we remain lovers all our marriage,' James said. 'As far as the main bedchamber, we can make that into a withdrawing room for you where you may entertain your guests. Can you not picture yourself in a new silk gown, talking of gaieties with a few intimate friends?'

Purity obediently tried, but the picture remained cloudy. Sir Joshua had never encouraged friendships and Ladymoon Manor was, in any case, too remote for people to drop in casually. Neither could she see herself sitting in her best gown for more than an hour. At this time of the year the bottling and preserving of fruit, the salting of meat and fish for the winter months would begin and there was little leisure for twiddling her thumbs.

Glancing at her husband she wondered, a little uneasily, if he had lived so long at Court that he had forgotten how ordinary folk went on.

The next day they rode to York. Purity had been ready to go on horseback with Aunt Hepzibah's coffin laid on the black painted wagon kept for such melancholy occasions, but James had insisted upon retaining the hired coach for themselves.

'Your father may have sold his

carriage because he seldom went visiting,' he said, 'but I have no intention of following his example. We must delay our return from York, my love, until we have provided ourselves with a neat carriage and a pair of well-matched greys.'

She had planned to spend the harvest profits on a new charcoal range, for in winter the wind blew so strongly down the wide kitchen chimney that the servants were constantly brushing soot out of their clothes. But James was right in his desire to live as befitted their station in life.

As the hired coach crested the moorland road and began the final run towards the grey walls of the city, her thoughts turned to the following wagon with its sad burden. This visit to York was, like the homecoming, very different from what she had imagined it would be.

In the churchyard she lingered, when the service was over, to look at the other tombstones. Her mother and father had separate graves and those were separated by the tombs of Elisha and Hope. Aunt Hepzibah had been a little shocked at that.

'For husbands and wives are generally laid together,' she had said, nervously twisting her hands.

'I'll not inflict my father on anyone even when he's dead,' Purity had answered wryly.

Mercy lay on the side next to her mother and next to her was the new grave, the ropes still coiled at the side of the piled turf, a solitary wreath of white roses hanging with a rakish air from the wooden cross that would be replaced, when the earth had settled, by a more permanent memorial.

At a little distance were buried the grandparents who had, after all, been no blood-kin. But they must have been good people to have taken in a gypsy foundling.

'Purity, I hope you will accept my condolences on the death of your aunt.' Benjamin Rathbone, whom she had glimpsed briefly in the church, had approached and was bowing to her.

'Thank you, Benjamin.' She bowed in return, her smile cordial.

'It was, I'm given to understand, very sudden.'

'But not entirely unexpected. But you must wish me joy too,' she said. 'I am newly married to Master James Rodale — he is over there, talking to the minister.'

'I heard a rumour,' he said, unsmiling. 'I hoped it was no more than that, but seeing you with a stranger, I feared it was true.'

'But you will wish me joy?' she persisted.

'I will wish you a measure of contentment,' he said reluctantly. 'Is it also true that he is a King's man?'

'Equerry to His Majesty,' she said. 'His duties will be much lighter now that he is married, of course, but he will be required to attend at Court from time to time.'

'I am sorry that you chose to disregard

your father's principles,' Benjamin said. 'It is, I know, none of my concern — '

'That's right!' she interrupted crossly.

'But I feel bound to say,' he continued inexorably, 'that I am deeply disappointed in your conduct. To refuse my own offer and to take instead a middle-aged rake — '

'And that's enough,' she said coldly. 'Don't ever presume to imagine that because you were married to my sister that gives you the right to dictate my actions! I'd hoped we might be friends, but I can see that is impossible.'

'Regrettably so.' He bowed again and walked away, the very picture of offended dignity.

'Are you ready to leave, sweetheart?' James was returning, his hat in his hand.

'Quite ready.' She gave him her warmest smile, wishing that Benjamin Rathbone had lingered to see it.

They returned to Ladymoon Manor the next day, having stayed overnight at a modest inn just within the city gates.

Purity had hoped that James might take her to see his parent's old house where he had spent his boyhood, but he had gone out alone, returning with the information that he had purchased both carriage and horses.

'At a ruinously expensive price, my darling! But you will look like a queen riding in it!'

He had kissed her boisterously and, smelling his breath, she guessed that the sale had been ratified over several drinks.

But it was certainly an elegant coach, she thought, when they stepped out into the cobbled yard the next morning. Of dove grey picked out in gold and white it presented a smartly trim appearance. Eben was running a practised hand over the flanks of the two beautifully matched greys and Jessie, coifed and cloaked for the journey, exclaimed in pleasure over the cushioned and padded interior.

'It was ordered by a rich widow over Scarborough way,' James explained, 'but the lady died and the whole equipage was up for sale again. You'll be the envy of the district!'

'We are already attracting a great deal of attention,' she murmured, glancing at the people who had lingered to stare. 'They will think I have come into a title or something.'

James began to answer but as suddenly appeared to change his mind, and, opening the door, thrust her up the step with so little ceremony that she gaped at him in astonishment.

'We'd best be starting back,' was all he said, and leaned to slam shut the door, barely giving Jessie time to follow her mistress.

As the greys trotted into the main street Purity caught a glimpse through the window of a tall man in a cocked hat who stood among the crowd. She might not have noticed him at all, for his dress was sober and his features undistinguished, were it not for the red hair that curled down to his shoulders. The brilliant hair would have marked him out at any gathering, and he seemed to take as much interest in her for his eyes narrowed in concentration as she glanced at him.

'That gentleman with red hair will know me if he sees me again,' she said lightly.

'I saw nobody,' James said. His voice was lazy, but he dabbed sweat from his temples as he made himself more comfortable beside her.

For no reason she could pin-point she began to feel uneasy. From then on it was as if, even when she was happiest, some long finger of shadow reached out to chill her.

Yet her life was quite different from anything she had known before. There was little room for loneliness when James was there, to eat dinner and supper with her, to tease her into playing cards and dice in the long evenings when they sat in the parlour together, to make her dress up in the gowns she had bought in London and lay aside her mourning dress.

As the winter drew on he encouraged her to remain indoors by the fire while he, mounted on one of the new greys, rode over to consult Eben on business matters.

'For you are far too pretty to bother your head with long columns of figures,' he said, kissing her, 'you should concentrate on making yourself beautiful and gay.'

'As if I were a doll,' she thought, but the thought was a tenderly mocking one. It was, after all, a very great thing to be so cherished.

'My love, will you be very unhappy if I leave you for a few days?' he enquired one morning.

'Leave me? Why, where are you going?' She looked up in surprise from her cup of chocolate.

Chocolate, according to James, was newly fashionable and so she drank it to please him, though it was too thick and sweet for her taste.

'With Christmas so near,' he explained, 'I wished to buy some gifts.'

'We could go together,' she began, but he put a finger to her lips saying, 'I'll wager that in Sir Joshua's day Christmas was not even observed, and I'll not have you spend more of your money on me.'

'Will you be away for long?' she asked.

'No more than two or three days. Nat can drive me in, for he's a good whip and handles the animals well. Would you like me to bring back anything for you? Cook was complaining the other day that she was running out of ginger.'

'Would you? There are several things we need.'

'For you, my darling wife, I would do anything,' he said.

'Except take me to York,' she thought, and again the faint finger of uneasiness pricked her mind.

'I'll ask Cook what she lacks,' she said aloud, and went through to the kitchen.

Cook, brooding over preserves in the

stillroom behind the kitchen, was ready with her list.

'Pepper, mace, nutmeg — oh, there's a deal of spices we need, mistress,' she said. 'Did you say Master Rodale was fetching them in?'

'He's going to York for a few days,' Purity told her.

'Ah, that'd be on account of the gentleman who called yesterday.' Cook wiped her hands on a damp rag and stood on tiptoe to examine the spice jars.

'Which gentleman?'

'The one who rode by to see Master Rodale. Oh, but you were over at Jessie's, so you'll not have seen him. He wasn't here more than a quarter of an hour and then he went off again.'

'Did he — he didn't, by chance, have red hair?' Purity asked.

'Red hair? No, mistress, not that I noticed.'

'No matter. I'll get these things brought back for you.'

Armed with her list she went back

into the parlour where James, having finished his breakfast, was putting on his boots.

'I'll shower Cook with every spice in creation,' he promised.

'You didn't tell me we'd had a visitor,' she said.

'Visitor?' For a moment he looked puzzled and then his brow cleared. 'Of course! You were over at Jessie's, weren't you? A man rode by to enquire if we had any ewes to sell. I told him we had not, and he rode away again.'

'How extraordinary!' She stared at him. 'Everybody knows the sheep are driven to market to be sold. What was his name, and why come here to make enquiry? Eben deals with all that.'

'His name was Ackers,' James said.

'Ackers I don't know a farmer of that name.'

'It might have been Ackers. His tones were so rustic I could have been mistaken. He seemed a foolish fellow, so I didn't trouble Eben with

246

the matter. Are you certain that's the whole list?'

'Yes. That's all.' She accepted his kiss, pushing further questions to the back of her mind.

'In three days, my darling. You do promise to take care of yourself?'

'Yes, of course.' She put her arms round his neck and rubbed her cheek against his, in a little, self-consciously female gesture. It was, she thought, the first time she had ever had to employ such arts, and the realisation saddened her a little.

The three days passed more slowly than she had imagined they would. She had quickly grown accustomed to having company and the days seemed very long. At this time the garden was at its least inviting and there was a threat in the rising wind.

Once she went into the prayer-chamber and took the golden cup from its hiding place. She had not confided its existence to anyone, even to James. Now, staring at the silver face, she decided that when they had been married for a year she would show it to her husband and together they would toast their twelve months of happiness. The thought of that was like a talisman to hold up against her growing doubts.

But when James returned with parcels piled up on the seat of the coach, her doubts evaporated like mist over the river. He had brought spices and rolls of silk and wool, some bottles of claret, and a pretty turquoise ring.

'For the ring we used at the wedding belonged to my mother. I wanted you to have something of your own.'

He slipped the ring on her finger, kissed the tip of her nose, and went whistling into the kitchen to give Cook and the two servant girls the woollen cloaks and bunches of gay ribbon he had brought back for them. Certainly his presence had made a great difference in the household. Unlike Sir Joshua James liked to hear the maids singing at their work and, since his arrival, the evening prayers had dwindled to no more than a thanks for the meal just eaten and a petition for the king's safety.

It was after Christmas that the letter came, and with it a deepening of the shadow. The festival itself had passed more merrily than Purity had ever known it to be.

Sir Joshua had regarded the season of Yuletide as an opportunity for more prayer and penitence, reminding his family that the Cross hung over the Stable and that present joy led only to tears. For the first time in her life Purity sat down to roast goose and a plum pudding flamed in cognac and swirled in cream. The gifts from York that James had brought were so extravagant that she almost brought out the golden cup, but at the last moment some instinct checked her. It was the same instinct that had made her keep her mother's gypsy origins to herself.

It was at the New Year that the message came, delivered by a carter who had received it from a pedlar. It was heavily sealed and addressed to Master James Rodale in a small, angular hand.

She carried it to James and waited, hands folded at her waist, as he broke the seals and read the thickly folded missive.

'Is something wrong?' Alarmed by his sudden pallor she put out her hand towards him, but he turned aside, crumpling the paper and tossing it into the blazing fire.

'Court duties,' he said briefly. 'I am required to attend upon His Majesty for the space of two weeks.'

'Do we go to London at once?' she asked.

'*We* don't go anywhere,' he said, his mouth displeased. 'I am bidden to attend alone.'

'Oh.' She stared at him blankly.

'Sweetheart, as you've not yet been officially presented at Court, it would be a gross breach of taste to take you there,' he said. 'I shall make enquiry, of course, so that you may be presented as soon as possible.'

'I could travel with you and stay quietly in private,' she suggested.

'My darling, when you come to Court you'll come as proudly as a princess and take your place there among the other ladies,' he said warmly. 'I'll not have my wife creep like a mouse.'

'I'd not mind,' she said wistfully, but he put his arm round her, declaring he would hear no more argument. Beyond him she could see the blackened edges of the letter curling into ash.

He left the next morning, taking Nat with him as coachman, and declaring that the weather was so mild he expected no difficulties along the road.

'And I will try to send word that I have arrived safely,' he promised.

'I shall clean the house and bake comfits ready for your return,' she said, hiding tears.

'Good little Roundhead!' he approved.

'But I am no longer a Roundhead,'

she thought when the coach had bowled away. 'And I am not at all certain if I'm good. Inside me, at this moment, is a seething rebellion and I don't know why I'm feeling like that. I have a husband whom I love, a beautiful home, and loyal servants, and I won't be thirty until next year.'

She took her cloak from its peg and went out impatiently into the garden. The crisp air caught at her throat and made her cough. Overhead the sky was the colour of pearl and the unleaved trees were black against it.

She walked restlessly, kicking at the ground with the tip of her shoe. If only she could walk away the endless three weeks that were ahead of her! When James was with her the uneasiness was no more than a murmur at the back of her mind.

There was a solitary rider moving away among the trees. She stopped short and gazed after him, wondering who it could be. Eben rode a brown mare, but this horse was black, its rider tall and thin. From beneath his hat his long red hair fell thick and straight to below the shoulders of his maroon coat.

He was too far away for her to call him, even had she wanted to do so. That it was the same man who had gazed at her in York was beyond question. She shivered, the air cold on her cheek, and turned back towards the house, wishing that James were there and knowing that even if he were she would have no idea what to ask him.

There were two letters from James in the weeks that followed, both delivered by the carter. She read them avidly, tracing the words with her finger. Aunt Hepzibah had done her best but Purity was uncomfortably aware that her education was sketchy. She had never completely mastered either reading or writing, though she could add up figures very swiftly, and her husband's letters were full of long, elegant words.

He was, she made out, missing her very greatly, and had decided to resign his post at Court, give up his apartment in Whitehall, and return north to lead the life of a country gentleman. In the second letter, delivered two weeks after the first, he wrote that the king had accepted his resignation and that he would be coming home as soon as possible.

'Jeremy, my servant, has agreed to forsake his native city and return with me. I confess that I have greatly missed his services in recent months. The rogue has acquired a wife since I left him to his own devices! Fortunately Adele has earned her living as a lady's maid and is, so Jeremy assures me, a wonder at dressing hair. She is also from Paris and so will know more about the latest fashions than a mere man. It would, I feel, be convenient if they could be given your aunt's rooms. They are small but could be made comfortable for them.'

Aunt Hepzibah had occupied those

rooms for more than thirty years without complaint, but no doubt London servants had much higher standards. Purity folded the letter carefully and put it away in the drawer. She supposed that it would be much more genteel to have two superior domestics, and certainly James was in need of a body-servant. She had heard him cursing in the mornings as he drew on his hose. As for herself, she decided ruefully that she would have to get used to having her hair dressed by a lady's maid from Paris. It was a shame that her new grandeur would not be seen in London, but now that James had resigned his appointment it was not likely she would ever be presented at Court.

Sighing, she went out to the kitchen to tell Janet that Aunt Hepzibah's rooms were to be aired and clean linen put on the bed.

Another week passed by before James returned. She had put on her best silk dress every evening in the hope of his arrival, but six long evenings dragged by before the rattle of harness and Nat's loud and cheerful greeting brought her from the fireside.

'Purity, my love!' James was already out of the coach and embracing her warmly.

'You ought to have sent word,' she said. 'We have grown tired of eating a specially prepared supper for next day's dinner each day!'

'You see how she pecks at me, Jeremy?' James turned to the man emerging from the coach.

'And no doubt you well deserve it, sir! Mistress, it gives me great pleasure to see you again.' He was bowing over her hand.

'I hope you'll be very happy here,' she said cordially.

'I'm sure I shall get used to it, mistress. London has been a dull place since the master left.'

'And the Court is dullest of all, for the Princess Mary's death ended much of the gaiety,' James said. 'But you have not greeted Adele, my love! You did receive my letter, telling you of Jeremy's rash plunge into matrimony?'

'Indeed I did and congratulate you both.' She held out her hand to the slim, cloaked figure who stood a little apart from the men.

'Good-evening, madame. I am most happy to be here.' The voice was low and husky with only the faintest hint of an accent. Purity had a brief glimpse in the light of the torch that Sally was holding, of a long, pale face framed in elaborate yellow curls.

'We cannot possibly stand out in this cold wind all night!' James was exclaiming. 'Shall we go into the parlour? You did see to the rooms, Purity?'

'Yes. They're quite ready.'

'And very warm and clean, you may be sure.' James put a hand on Jeremy's shoulder. 'My little Roundhead is a marvellous housekeeper.'

He was steering them through the

door, calling over his shoulder to Nat to bring in the luggage.

'I am so glad you are home,' Purity said, smiling brightly into the flaring light of the torch.

9

'I always feel at ease in this house,' Purity said, leaning back in the comfortable, high-backed chair and smiling across at Jessie.

'It's thanks to you, mistress, that we have such a grand home,' Jessie said gratefully. 'Snug and dry as a palace it is, and Eben plans to have the garden laid out and ready for planting within the month.'

'It ought to be lovely by the time the roses are cut. You must take some cuttings.'

'Thank you kindly.' Jessie shifted slightly on her own chair, then said. 'Talking of roses, mistress, there are none in your own cheeks these days, if you'll excuse my mentioning it. You're not sick?'

'I'm perfectly well,' Purity said quickly.

'I thought — ladies do often lose their colour when they're with child.'

'I'm not having a child.' Purity bit her lip and blurted nervously. 'It is not fitting for me to say this to you, but it does take two people to make a child. My husband does not — visit me as often as he formally did.'

'You sleep apart still?'

'As you know, we've done so from the beginning. It is the new fashion.'

'I never heard of such a fashion,' Jessie said. 'Why, bedding is more than a matter of rutting, mistress. There's warmth in it, and closeness, and talking over the day.'

'He seldom comes to me at night,' Purity repeated. 'Perhaps I expect too much, make too many demands.'

'More likely he cannot keep two women satisfied,' Jessie said.

'That cannot be.' Purity rose in agitation and walked over to the window.

'Don't say it never entered your own head, mistress,' Jessie spoke respectfully but firmly. 'Why, it's been clear to Eben and me for a long time ever since that Jeremy and his wife came riding back from London. I'll wager they sleep separate too.'

'It is the fashion,' Purity said.

Her hand, straying to the curtain, pleated it carefully, but the pattern on the material blurred before her eyes.

'And if you believe that, you'll believe anything,' Jessie said angrily. 'I'm sorry, mistress, but you did bring up the subject, and I must speak my mind. I've been servant to the Makins since I was a little lass, and you and I are much of an age. Your father was a hard, unloving man but he was honest, and he never brought another woman into the house after your mother died. Master Rodale has lived too long at Court and picked up southern ways.'

'I know nothing for certain.' Purity stopped pleating the curtain and swung around, her face pleading. 'I could prove nothing and I may be wrong. It is only that she is young and comely, and there is something in the way she and James look at each other, as if they had a secret and were laughing inside.'

'Why don't you dismiss them?' Jessie asked.

'My husband employs them.'

'On your money.' Jessie spoke with embarrassment. 'I know that's none of my concern either, but since Master Rodale took to going over the books with Eben, he's been borrowing already on next season's profits.'

'It's not really a wife's business, to add profit and loss,' Purity said.

'Perhaps it isn't,' Jessie agreed, 'but when a husband has extravagant tastes and not much head for figures, then it's for the wife to act. I'm sorry to speak so plain, mistress, but I've a great fondness for you, and I don't like to see you cheated on all sides.'

'I'll have to think.' She shook her head slightly as if to contradict her own thoughts. 'Jeremy seems to notice nothing but he pays a little attention to his wife. He's always very polite to me, but I cannot imagine myself ever talking to him as I talk to you and Eben.'

'London manners,' Jessie scorned. 'All froth and no kindness! You're too forebearing, mistress.'

'I'll see what's to be done.' She cast another look round the warm, pleasantly appointed room. 'You'll not speak of this, Jessie?'

'Not even to Eben.' Jessie came over and laid her hand briefly on Purity's arm. 'You'll visit us again, soon?'

'You'd be hard put to it to keep me away,' Purity said.

Remounting in the yard beyond which a garden was taking shape, she forced a bright smile as she waved farewell. Two of Jessie's younger children were playing ball nearby and their shouts rang through the air. That was what was lacking at Ladymoon Manor, Purity thought. Children ought to be running about in the garden or coming indoors with laughing faces and muddy shoes. The house was too large and too quiet, and despite the new coach and horses, she and James never went anywhere or entertained any visitors. Yet their times alone together were few, for James liked to sit up late, playing cards or dice with Jeremy, and their talks were usually interrupted by James declaring he was weary of serious conversation, and wanted Adele to entertain them with one of the French ballads she sang in a breathless, off-key little voice that irritated Purity beyond endurance, but which James seemed to find enchanting.

As she rode homeward Purity's mind returned to the previous evening. She had felt tired and listless for much of the day as she sometimes did at this season of the year. James however had been in a lively, cordial mood, insisting that Jeremy and Adele be invited to join them in the larger of the two parlours.

'Jeremy can play a pretty flute,' he

said, 'and Adele will show you how to dance the latest dance from Paris.'

'I cannot even dance the latest dance from England!' Purity exclaimed.

'Poor darling! Your education has been grossly mishandled,' he teased. 'Tell Janet to bring some wine up from the cellar and I wager you'll be leaping with the best of them before the moon is up!'

She went obediently to give the orders to Janet and returned to the parlour, carrying her sewing with her, for experience had taught her that such evenings usually ended with herself sitting neglected in the corner.

On James's insistence she had relinquished her mourning and wore a gown of soft blue silk ruched with lace. The material had been one of his Christmas gifts to her, and Adele had made it into a becoming dress. It was unfortunate that the colour made Purity's complexion look even sallower than usual, and the lace cuffs were slightly too long, hiding her slender fingers. She had meant to alter it herself, but now, watching Jeremy's yellow-curled wife in her gown of pale ivory with bunches of lilac ribbon that darkened Adele's eyes to sapphire she felt a small clutch of despair. She could never hope to look as elegant as the Parisian girl, and at that moment nobody could have imagined that Adele was only the maid.

'You look dismal, sweetheart,' James said, flicking her cheek with his finger. 'That Roundhead conscience is not pricking you because we plan a little gaiety, is it?'

She shook her head, wishing he would not call her that. Once it had sounded tender. Now it sounded mocking and his glance had already slid away from her towards Jeremy's wife.

'Then we'll show you how the galliard is stepped in the Courts of Europe. Play, Jeremy!'

He had moved over to Adele and was bowing before her. Jeremy had taken the flute from its case and was fingering its smooth surface. In a moment a tune filled the room and Adele was on her feet, her ivory skirt billowing, her golden head bent as she sank into a curtsey. In a moment more they were dipping and swaying up and down the room.

'You make a handsome couple!' Purity called as the dance drew to its end. She was aware that her voice held a quality of forced generosity and was ashamed of it.

'I flatter myself that I chose a lovely little wife, mistress,' Jeremy said. 'She is of an excellent family, you know.'

'You married above your station,' James said. 'Adele needs no reference from you, my friend. Come Purity, do you think you can manage the steps? Jeremy will play more slowly and you will have only to follow my lead.'

'I have never danced,' she said helplessly but allowed herself to be led into the centre of the room.

To dance with her husband ought to have been a pleasure. She kept telling herself that as she tried to remember the intricate dips and turns of the measure, but she was uncomfortably aware that her movements were clumsy, her feet could not tap out the steps in time with the chords of the music, and she held her head at the wrong angle.

'My love, you're doing quite splendidly!' James cried.

Glancing up she saw that his eyes were straying still towards Adele and this time there was no mistaking the mockery in them.

'I really would prefer to sit and watch,' she said, her voice high and thin. 'Indeed I have a very bad headache, and the music and wine make it worse. Would you mind very much if I retired early?'

'I will attend you, madame,' Adele said promptly.

'No need. I am accustomed to undress myself,' Purity said.

'Shall I brew a tisane for you, mistress?' Jeremy asked. 'I have some skill in the mixing of remedies.'

'I'm in no need of any remedy save rest,' she said sharply. 'No, James, don't stop the dancing on my account. The music won't disturb me at all.'

She smiled brightly at him, her lips achingly stiff, her eyes shadowed by her dark lashes.

'Goodnight then, sweetheart.' James kissed her lightly, his hand warm on her shoulder, his foot already tapping the floor again as Jeremy raised the flute to his lips. Just as she closed the door she heard Adele begin to laugh.

Thinking of that now she tightened her grip on the reins and spurred her mare onward.

The moors wore their spring time green, flashed here and there with pale cowslips and opening blossoms of gorse. As she neared the manor house another rider swerved towards her from among the trees.

She frowned when she saw who the horseman was, but drew rein and waited, erect in the saddle as he reached her.

'Mistress Purity, I wish you good-day.'

'Good-day, Benjamin.' She returned the greeting coldly.

'I hope you are well.'

'Perfectly well. You surely haven't ridden all the way out here to enquire about my health?'

'I have always had a strong interest in your welfare,' Benjamin told her.

'You need not concern yourself with that, for I do very well,' she said, making to ride on, but his hand gripped her bridle.

'I must speak to you,' he said, his heavy face sombre. 'I really must insist that I talk to you.'

'I wish you'd let me alone,' she said, jerking free. 'Surely I made it clear when we last met that I wished all communications to be ended between us.'

'Either I talk to you or to the sheriff at York,' he said.

'The sheriff? Why on earth should you want to talk to the sheriff?' she demanded.

'If you would step down for a moment, I'll explain,' he said.

'It had best be a good explanation,' she said grimly, dismounting and scowling at him.

'I beg you to believe that I have your interests at heart,' he began, dismounting in his turn. 'Your sister and I were very happily married, and my own offer to you was prompted by genuine affection.'

'Yes, very well. The subject is closed now.'

'Not entirely. I would still be very willing to make you my wife,' he said.

'As I am now married the question doesn't arise.'

'It is of your marriage that I wish to speak,' he told her.

'And that, like my health, is none of your concern,' she snapped.

'James Rodale is not what you believe him to be,' Benjamin said.

'Is any man?' She spoke lightly, her eyes dangerous.

'You know nothing about him.'

'I know sufficient. He was born and bred a Yorkist, and had some acquaintance with my mother when both were young.'

'That much is true,' he said grudgingly. 'But his family left York years before, at about the same time your mother was wed. Since then he has been something of an adventurer.'

'No harm in that,' she retorted. 'When the war came he fought for the king. I cannot recall you doing the same for Parliament!'

'I had a business to run. He had turned his hand to no profession and squandered his father's money.'

'He went into exile for nine years,' Purity said, wondering why she had troubled to argue. 'That is not a little thing! While you were growing fat on your profits and trying to breed heirs in my poor sister, James was wandering the courts of Europe.'

'I'll grant him a certain loyalty to his own side,' he said.

'For which he was rewarded,' she said proudly. 'Equerry to the king.'

'Equerry to nobody,' Benjamin said flatly.

'You don't seem to know that I met him at Whitehall, in attendance upon the king,' she said triumphantly.

'I have just returned from London,' Benjamin said. 'I made enquiries there — '

'You had no right,' she interrupted, but his voice carried on relentlessly.

'Enquiries about Master James Rodale Equerry to King Charles the Second. There is no record in the Household List of any such Equerry. There is no record of any James Rodale. The only James Rodale anyone could recall was an impoverished Yorkshire Royalist who earned a living by his wits.'

'He stood within the ropes, near to the king's table,' she said chokingly.

'Had you paid extra for your ticket you could have stood there with him,' he said. 'It confers no special privilege, to pay more for a ticket. It simply gives you the chance to see more plainly what the king is eating for dinner.'

'He had an apartment — a grace and favour apartment — in the Palace, and a body-servant — '

'Called Jeremy? A Cockney rogue who earned a living renting out doxies to gentlemen with more money than sense. The pair were known as a couple of amiable scoundrels.'

'But the apartment — '

'Rooms can be rented at the Palace. It is another way of increasing the king's revenue without troubling Parliament for a loan.'

'James may not be quite everything he claimed to be,' she said carefully. 'He may have — stretched the truth a little. He's proud and wouldn't want me to believe that I was marrying a poor man.'

'My dear, he never married you at all,' Benjamin said.

'Now I know you've run mad,' she

said scornfully. 'At least give me credit for knowing if I was at my own wedding or not!'

'Was it not a speedy affair,' he asked, 'with a minister hastily summoned from his bed?'

'Yes it was. How did you know?'

'Such weddings take place often these days,' he said. 'They have no legality at all, but silly young girls are duped by them into giving up their virginity.'

'James had a special licence.'

'Sealed with a fine crest? The licence comes with the minister and one is as false as the other.'

'But why make such a pretence? Why not marry me in truth?' she asked in bewilderment.

'Because in the Year of Grace, sixteen-hundred and fifty-seven, Master James Rodal was wed in Paris to a certain Adele Dubonnet, mantle maker. There are men at Court who drank healths at that marriage and will swear to it if necessary.'

It was true. Even his obvious

satisfaction at being the one to break the news could not disguise the fact that it was true. She heard herself say in a prim little voice, 'I see you have been very busy about my affairs.'

'I came to see you, to soften the blow,' he told her. 'If you wish to return with me to York we can lay information against the three of them.'

'Give me leave to think.' She walked a few steps and stood with head bent, pondering.

It was odd but she felt no real shock. It was as if she had always known that James could not have remained faithful for so many years to a girl he had met briefly only twice.

'I never knew my mother,' she said in a low voice, 'for she died when I was born. Aunt Hepzibah told me once that she was gentle and unloved. But James knew her when they were boy and girl, before her hopes were stifled in a loveless marriage. Perhaps, in loving him, I was trying to live the life my own mother would have led, had things been different.'

'Will you go with me to York?' Benjamin asked.

'For what reason?' She turned to face him, a curious blankness in her eyes. 'The ceremony I went through was false, no more than a jest.'

'He made you believe that it was a real one!'

'Perhaps I knew it was a jest all along. Perhaps it amuses me to pretend to be the wife when I am really the mistress.'

'You know that isn't true,' he said. 'You would not so dishonour yourself, not with your rearing.'

'Ah, yes, my father was an honourable man,' Purity nodded. 'All his life he acted for the best. He sent his eldest son to war to die gloriously for Parliament. He drove his other son to cheating and stealing, and his daughter to the river, and he treated Mercy and me as household slaves. And when he died the minister spoke of his high principles and stern devotion to duty!

Well, I can do without such principles and such devotion.'

'James Rodale is not your husband!' Benjamin said.

'But he is still my lover. Not very often, but now and then he still comes to me at night, telling me how much he loves me, and at such times I wouldn't care if he had a dozen real wives.'

'You are immoral, as licentious as he is,' Benjamin said in horror.

'Then be thankful that I never accepted your proposal of marriage,' she said.

'I would not dream of renewing that offer,' he said stiffly. 'Indeed I shall try to forget that it was ever made.'

'How very wise of you!' Her tone was as mocking as James's eyes had been when he glanced past her to where Adele sat in her ivory gown.

'I wish you good-day, Mistress Purity.'

He put a sarcastic emphasis upon the last word, then mounted and rode away without looking back.

There were tears on her cheeks. It was natural, she excused herself, that she should weep a little for the betrayal she had suffered. Yet nothing was ever completely evil. James had deceived her, but he was kind and attentive, and she had reached the age when she could bear to close her mind to anything that threatened its peace.

She was in the orchard, not very far from the house. Calling to Dickon to take the horse she made her way through the side-gate into the garden. Spring was all about her here and smoke belched cheerfully from the chimneys above the crouching eaves.

Inside, the rooms wore their quiet, afternoon aspect. The kitchen door was closed but she could hear the faint strains of Jeremy's flute and Sally's voice raised in song. The manservant often amused the maids for an hour or two, and she had wondered why Adele had never displayed any jealousy of his flirtatiousness. Now it was all clear to her, and a wry smile curved her lips.

In the space of ten minutes the eager, romantic girl had grown into a woman mature enough not only to take second best but to accept the fact without too much bitterness.

She went gently up the stairs with the intention of changing her habit for a lighter gown. Adele, whatever she might be to James, had proved valuable at dressing hair. Purity touched the glossy blackness of her own braids and stopped short as voices drifted to her from the partly open door of Aunt Hebzibah's room.

'Taking a risk.' That was Adele's husky tone.

'She'll not be back until supper time. When she and Jessie Rowe get together they clack away the time in gossip.'

That was James, indulgent and amused. She moved closer, poised for flight at the foot of the short staircase.

'Nat says there are gypsies no more than two miles away. Perhaps they will steal her and we'll not see her again.'

Adele sounded hopeful.

'They'd not touch one of their own,' James said.

'One of their own?' The husky voice was puzzled.

'Her mother was part gypsy, a foundling adopted by a couple in York. They passed her off as the child of a dead cousin, and it was never questioned, for she was fair and blue-eyed.'

'Like me?' The voice was a little jealous.

'Yoni was comely enough,' James said carelessly. 'I even had it in mind to wed her at one stage. Then my mother ferretted out the truth of her birth, and I was glad I hadn't asked for her hand.'

'But she knew,' Purity thought in a cold anguish. 'She knew why he hadn't asked her. That was why she entered into a loveless match.'

'But you have a fondness for the daughter.' The voice was definitely accusing now.

'Don't be a goose! Purity is useful

281

to me, always has been useful. She's an innocent, locked up in her fairy tale world of escaping Royalists and love come true after a long absence.'

'You are kind to her,' Adele grumbled.

'Kindness costs nothing,' he said. 'And you suffer very little from the few attentions I pay her.'

'I am dull here. It is so much gayer in Paris, or in London. Here we do nothing.'

'Wait until we find the cup,' James said. 'As soon as we find that we'll be away from her.'

'Bah! There is no cup!' Adele said angrily. 'It is all a big tale, no more than that.'

'A tale that has lasted for more than a generation. My father was a lawyer who acted for the old woman who used to own Ladymoon Manor. Old Mistress Bainbridge was half crazy and rambled on a lot, but there was definitely a cup here. A golden cup with a woman's face engraved on it in silver.'

'But you have not seen this cup yourself.'

'I've heard my father mention it, and I've a feeling it exists. I've a feeling it's still here.'

'But, my darling, you cannot tear down the walls.'

'I can persuade my little Roundhead to have some alterations done and carry her off to Buxton until the house is straight again. Jeremy and you will remain here to supervise the workmen.'

'Where is this Buxton?'

'It's a spa, my love. Elderly gentlemen, like myself, go there to take the waters and renew their youth.'

'I wish to come with you,' she said promptly.

'I want you to stay here. Somebody has to remain here to watch Jeremy, for if the cup is found his loyalty to me may be swallowed up in greed.'

'And Jeremy will watch me?'

'You're a clever girl!' His voice was amused and approving.

'You will fall in love with her,'

Adele said gloomily. 'You will go to this Buxton place and you will fall in love with her.'

'My darling, I'd as soon fall in love with Janet or Sally — sooner, for they are good-looking, lively girls. Purity is too much of a Roundhead to enjoy life, and the gypsy strain is evident in her face. She's a throwback to some Romany hag with a tattered shawl and brass rings in her ears.'

If she heard any more she would burst in and denounce them, the hurt and humiliation pouring out of her in a torrent.

There had been no truth in him from the beginning. He had spurned her mother and now, years later, had grasped his opportunity to get back into Ladymoon Manor, not simply to enjoy the profits, but to search for the cup he believed was hidden there.

She moved silently away, down the main staircase, through the hall and the small parlour into the garden again. She held herself stiffly and she was so cold that her bones ached. She supposed that when one was dead the same cold would invade her, but surely in death there would be some end to the wrenching pain.

'Are you riding out again, mistress?' Dickon enquired.

'I only called in to get something.'

It was peculiar, being able to speak when she was in such pain.

'I've not unsaddled her, mistress. I was off in a dream thinking how bonny the new flowers look.' Dickon had a sweetheart over Weston way and sneaked off to see her whenever he could.

'You can pick some and take them to Martha the next time you visit her,' Purity said.

'That's very good of you, mistress. She likes a few flowers to cheer up the place.' The groom's face had brightened.

Mounted again, she looked down at him, envying him his uncomplicated love, his simple nature that had never met a betrayal of the heart.

'Be about your work now,' she said, and touched her crop lightly to the horse's flanks. It cantered away into the green springtime of the moor and she felt the wind whip her icy cheek into a parody of living.

'I've been such a fool!' she cried aloud. 'I really believed he loved me and Ladymoon and intended to stay. I'd have pretended for the rest of my life that I didn't know the truth. I truly would have let matters go on. But even his lies have other lies behind them!'

She wanted to be dead like all the rest of her family, but it was not easy to die. And if she found the courage who would look after Ladymoon Manor? James would tear it stone from stone in order to find the cup.

A thin ripple of relief ran through her. She had been wise to follow her instincts and keep the existence of the cup to herself. It must, she thought, have been the strain of gypsy blood that had given her the instinct; the despised blood that had caused James to reject any idea of marrying her mother.

Adele had said there were gypsies camped at a little distance. They were bolder these past months because the new king had made it known that he found them amusing so that open persecution had ceased, and the smoke of their fires had drifted lazily across the horizon for several of the winter months.

She wheeled the mare in the direction she had last noticed the smoke and, with a new resolve in her expression, cantered towards it. The gypsies knew their own, James had said. That was why, on that other occasion, the old woman had stopped the men from robbing and harming her. God grant they would be ready to help their own!

The wagons and skin tents were circled in a hollow. She breasted the rise and drew rein, staring down at the gaudily painted vehicles and the rough-haired ponies cropping the short grass.

The Romanies must indeed be feeling secure. She could see a number of men lounging about and some children were playing with a dog.

As she rode down the slope towards them the tall woman, whom she recognised immediately as the one who had looked at her palm on that other occasion, rose from the step of one of the wagons and came forward, her craggy face impassive.

'You've no business here, mistress,' she said loudly.

'I've help to seek from my mother's people,' Purity said.

'Your mother was taken and reared in a house, and she has no claim upon us.'

'I will pay you well,' Purity said.

The haggard face grew sharper, the eyes flickering.

'You must want help badly,' the woman said. 'Step down and we'll talk.'

Stepping down, Purity felt the wrenching of pain again, but this time she was glad of it. Pain made it easier for her to nurture her anger.

An hour later she was on her way home again. She was not certain, as she jogged along the winding road, if her decision had been the right one. Perhaps James did have some affection for her that he had not cared to admit to his real wife.

'Fool!' she cried aloud, and lashed her mount with a sudden and unusual ferocity that caused the startled animal to plunge forward.

The sun was setting and below the blood-stained sky, colour was draining from the world.

'I wondered where on earth you were, my love,' James said as she came into the parlour.

'Gossipping with Jessie.' She bent to kiss him. 'You know what females are like when they get together.'

'You ought to take Jeremy with you when you ride out on the moor,' he said. 'There are gypsies camped in the neighbourhood, I'd not have you hurt or frightened by them.'

'I don't think they'd trouble to attack me. Where's Adele?'

'Upstairs, I suppose, laying out your dress for the evening. You're not going to sit down to supper in your riding-habit, sweetheart?'

'No, indeed. Tonight I want to look very gay and as lovely as Nature will allow.'

'Which is a surpassing degree of beauty!' He took her hand and pressed a kiss into the palm.

Looking down at the grey-blond head she thought, 'I still could love him, still bring myself to accept all this and go on as we did before. If only he would stay and not leave me.'

10

'That was a splendid supper!' James, sinking into a chair by the parlour fire, gave a comfortable belch.

'Cook has a light hand with pastry,' Purity said.

'And if I eat much more I shall swell like a pig's bladder.'

'You have a fine figure for a man of your years, sir,' Jeremy said promptly.

'A man of my years, forsooth! You talk as if I'd one foot in the grave!' James exclaimed.

'You are both fine men,' Purity said, 'and wise ones too — in taking young wives, I mean. Don't you agree with me, Adele?'

'Yes, madame.'

'You see, Adele has good sense too,' Purity said. 'A wise servant always agrees with her mistress.'

'You're very witty this evening.'

James gave her a faintly puzzled look.

'I am not always dull,' she smiled back.

'My love, I never thought you were,' he said quickly, 'and the Lord knows you've had sufficient cause. This place is not the liveliest in the world. Indeed I've been wondering if a change might do us both good.'

'How so?'

'The air at Buxton. The waters too, are said to be most healthful. We could take a trip there, stay for two or three weeks. Eben can safely be left in charge of the spring lambing.'

'It would be pleasant.' She folded her hands and gave him an eager look.

'We could have some painting and repanelling done while we're away,' he said. 'It would be pleasant to come back to a shining house, would it not?'

'Perhaps, in a week or two.' She gave him another eager, innocent look.

'We'll talk of it tomorrow. What is it to be tonight, Jeremy? Shall we roll the dice and enable me to win back a few of the coins you took from me last week?'

'I have a plan of my own,' Purity said.

'You wish to learn another of the Court dances, my love?' He gave her a sweet, tolerant smile.

'No, I shall leave the dancing to Adele. A wise mistress never competes with her maid,' she said demurely.

'Did you have something else in mind?' He gave her another patient smile.

'A story and a game,' she nodded. 'I will begin the tale and then we'll end it with a game.'

'Is it a riddle?' Adele asked.

'More like a mummers' play,' Purity said sweetly. 'Do sit down, Jeremy. The fire needs no more kindling and we have enough candles to illuminate Whitehall Palace. Did you know I met my husband there, Adele, after a nine year separation that grieved us both exceedingly?'

'Our private affairs are really not very interesting,' James said.

'And the gentry don't discuss private affairs with the servants, do they? But Jeremy and Adele are not like the usual servants, are they?'

'What about this story?' James asked.

'Ah, the story! It's an exciting one, James, and a sad one too, all about a gypsy girl who married a man she didn't love. Nobody knew she had Romany blood because some kind people had taken her in and reared her, and she had yellow hair and blue eyes. She must have looked a little like you, Adele. I hope you know who your parents really were, lest you chance to have Romany blood, and then James wouldn't like you at all.'

'Purity, you've been drinking,' James said.

'Not a drop, my love,' she reassured him. 'But later on I intend to celebrate. For the moment do let me go on with my tale.'

'I cannot understand it,' Adele said.

'Be patient and you will,' Purity said. 'This girl married, as I told you, and went to live with her husband in a house he had just bought. An old house, built on the foundations of an even older house that stood when the Romans were here. She bore five children here, without love, and died of the last of them. It was a girl, that youngest one. She had black hair and dark eyes and a sallow skin. In fact you could have set her down in any Romany camp without anyone thinking her out of place.'

'I cannot see the point of all this,' James said, his voice querulous.

'The girl grew up in the big house,' Purity went on, ignoring him. 'She was reared by the father who loved her as little as he had loved her gypsy mother. And then one day in the midst of a war that split brother from brother a man came, and the girl saw him for a little while and loved him ever afterwards.'

'Purity, for God's sake!' James had risen, his face suffused.

'But this is a comical tale,' Purity said, 'not a tragic one! The man came back once more, you see, and loved the girl. For just one night, you know, he truly loved her. She should have been content with that one night and let him go, but she was greedy as all females are, and she wanted that one night to be repeated for the rest of her life. So when the war ended she went to look for him.'

'And found him, and they were married, and lived happily ever after. Your tale is charming.'

James came over and bent to kiss her, but she rose, avoiding his touch, and stood facing them, her voice clear.

'You have not heard the comical part yet. The girl was a fool, you see, and believed what the man told her, believed him when he said they were wed. She was not to know that the licence had been false, and the minister a sham, and that he already had a real wife even younger than she was and able to dance all the

Court dances without falling over her own feet!'

There was a bleak silence. Adele's face had whitened, but Jeremy was as scarlet as his master. Then James, his voice shaking, said, 'You have some idea in your head. It is all nonsense, of course, but you may as well spill it out and be done!'

'Enquiries have been made,' she said levelly, 'so it's useless for you to go on denying things. You were never Equerry to the king or to anyone else, and you had no permanent apartment at Whitehall! You're one of dozens of impoverished Royalists who hang about on the fringes of the Court and try to scrape a living by their wits. I think you might have gone on doing that, contriving to remain just within the law, but then you saw me again.'

'And realised I still loved you,' he said swiftly.

'Learned from me that my father had died, making me his sole heir. You saw your chance and you took it,

James. A candlelit supper, a romantic secret wedding, a speedy return north — and how was I to know the room was rented, the marriage a counterfeit? And there you were with a handsome house and a docile wife, and even the possibility of stumbling upon a valuable cup that your father had once talked about.'

'He believed it might have been stolen away,' he said defensively.

'But the possibility of it still being here existed. And you had the house and the use of all the profits from the wool. You are in a most fortunate position!'

'Not entirely so,' he said sulkily. 'There was always the danger that someone might discover — '

'The man with red hair,' she remembered. 'Did he discover the truth?'

'That was a piece of ill fortune!' James exclaimed. 'I'd met the fellow only once or twice, but Adele was with me, and when he recognised me in York with a different lady he set to work to discover more, and he has been soliciting 'loans', as he calls them, ever since.'

'Which you pay so that he will keep quiet? I see.' What she saw was ugly and shabby and might have pained her had she not been so empty.

'I did not intend to bring Jeremy or Adele to Ladymoon Manor,' James said, 'but she would not remain in London.'

'So you received a summons to Court and, having resigned a position you never even held, came home with two extra servants!'

'A wife's place is with her husband,' Adele said.

'And you were even willing to share him from time to time with me. Generous!'

'What will you do?' James asked. 'Or have you already sent word to the authorities?'

'That is where the game begins,' Purity said. It was odd, feeling herself grow more cool and confident as the man she loved dwindled into a trickster.

'Game' He spoke uneasily.

'A very interesting game! I'll wager you never played it at Court!' she said with a kind of desperate gaiety.

'I don't understand,' Adele said helplessly.

'I'll explain it to you,' Purity said kindly.

She turned aside to the high cabinet and opened the lower door, stooping to lift out a small tray on which three glasses of red wine were arranged.

'You must agree that the situation has to be changed,' she said. 'You cannot expect to go on living here with a wife who pretends to be your mistress and a mistress who passes herself off as your wife?'

'So what is this game?' he asked.

'Three in a bed never prospered,' Purity said. 'A man can live happily with his wife, and he can live happily with his mistress. Two women can make shift to live together comfortably even when both have loved the same man. What I'm saying, my dear, is that one of us will have to leave.'

'And who is to decide?' James asked in astonishment.

'Jeremy will decide,' she said. 'He will decide which glass of wine each of us is to drink.'

'Are the glasses marked in some way?' James peered at them suspiciously.

'They contain excellent Burgundy,' she told him. 'You bought it yourself, when you went down to London. One of the glasses has an added ingredient. In spring it is possible to find foxgloves in the hollow of the moor. Henbane too and aconite.'

She smiled at them placidly, watching their faces change as realisation dawned.

'Are you saying,' James said at last, 'that one of those drinks contains poison?'

'I may be the one who drinks it,' said Purity. 'If so, then you may continue to live here, and in a year or so, why you can marry Adele all over again. Or Adele may be the one, and then it will be you and me at Ladymoon Manor, or you may drink it yourself. If that happens, then I will be the grieving widow with a devoted maidservant.'

'You *are* insane!' James said, sinking into the chair she had just vacated. 'If one of us died, the others might well be arrested for murder.'

'That's a risk for the living,' Purity said. 'The best games have more than one hazard. Jeremy here might very well be persuaded to declare that the poor deceased was low-spirited before mixing the drink. Come now, what do you say?'

'I will drink nothing,' Adele said shrilly. 'I will not play this game!'

'Have you no stomach for it, James?' Purity taunted him softly. 'Are you not man enough to take the risk of losing your life, or do you, after all, love her more than your hope of Ladymoon or me? Or does my Romany blood offend you as my mother's offended you long years ago, when there were cherries in November? Have you left your manhood in the Courts of Europe, James, along with your honour?'

'If you allow us to leave,' he said chokingly, 'I swear we will never trouble you again.'

'Perhaps I have already sent word to the Sheriff,' Purity mocked. 'I rode over to Jessie's today. I may have sent Eben to York and he may be on the way back with the constables at this moment. I wonder what the penalty is for your particular crime.'

'I am too old to go to prison,' James said.

'Too old to keep two women satisfied as well,' she said cruelly. 'But there is always the possibility that Adele or I might drink the wrong drink, and then you have one woman to please and Ladymoon Manor into the bargain.'

'You are insane,' he repeated. 'You should be locked in a Bedlam.'

'I was never more sane,' she said calmly. 'After all it's for you to choose.'

'To drink or not to drink?' He stared grey-faced, at the trio of glasses.

'Jeremy will see the game is fair,' she said. 'Come now, if you're a gambling man, you'll agree to take a small risk.'

'I wish to leave.' Adele had risen and was staring in terror from one to the other of them. 'I will not remain in this house! I will not remain.'

'If you choose you may all leave,' Purity said. 'There are three horses saddled in the stables and gold in the saddle bags. Leave now and I'll not press charges against any of you.'

'And if we choose to stay?' said James.

It was a vain attempt at belligerence, but his face was drained and defeated. In that moment he looked older than his years. She would have respected him more had he used violence or dared her to do the worst. Much as she had disliked her father at least he had been a man whose ruthlessness could be respected.

'Then we may play the game and choose to drink,' she said.

'And if we don't choose?'

'Then Eben goes to York, if he is not already on his way back from there, with company.'

In the corner of the room the clock ticked remorselessly. A log settled more cosily into its glowing bed. The others were frozen into their attitudes as if a spell had been laid upon them. Purity waited, holding the emptiness inside herself.

'I'll not take the risk,' James said at last. 'Not even for Ladymoon Manor, my dear. And certainly not for the sake of your bright eyes. I thought you mild and stupid, and I was fond of you. You may not believe that, but I was truly fond of you. And I would not have willingly hurt you. That's the truth.'

'No, it's not the truth,' she said wearily, 'but it's not important now. Either play the game or take the London road.'

Adele was clinging to him in tears,

her pretty face swollen, her long yellow curls disarranged. James put his arm about her and helped her to her feet. As they went slowly from the parlour Jeremy rose from his stool, where he had been observing the proceedings with bright interest, and drew his flute from his sleeve.

'You will need something, mistress, to cheer you in the long evenings ahead,' he told her as he bowed and followed them.

For a moment she stood irresolute, listening to the ticking of the clock. Then she went out into the hall. The door was ajar and she stood for a little while on the threshold, listening to the jangle of harness, to the thudding of hoofs that grew fainter as they receded.

'He did not even trouble to say good-bye,' Purity said aloud.

The garden was bathed in moonlight and there was no wind. On such a night Hope had gone down to the river to seek her lost love beneath the dark water. Purity walked slowly across the lawns, past the borders of night-scented stock and sweet basil, past the high hedge beyond which the blossom decked apple trees made lace patterns against the sky.

Beyond the gate the land sloped down to the river. Ribbons of moonlight twisted the waves that lapped the fern-fringed banks. Stark among the high, weed-tangled grass reared the stone columns and broken arches of the ancient convent.

'Ladymoon Manor was built from the stones of that convent,' the gypsy had told her. 'It was built for greed's sake and love turns sour there.'

'But I do love him,' Purity had said. 'I could still forgive, if only he loved me a little.'

'If he loves you,' the woman said, 'he will drink a glass of the wine, or even send the Frenchwoman away. If he loves you — '

But he had done neither of those things. Instead he had chosen to ride the London road, with his saddle-bags heavy with gold coin, and the woman who was his true wife at his side.

'I want no bodies left to tell tales,' Purity had said. 'The horses and the gold are yours, but the riders must not be found. Do you give me your word on that?'

'For the sake of your mother's blood and the insult offered it so long ago,' the gypsy said. 'We'll wait one night only on the London road. No longer.'

'If no riders pass that way,' Purity said, 'you may take it that we played the game.'

'I'll not order the attack if there are fewer than three riders,' the other warned.

'So let it be. I'm grateful.'

'Keep your gratitude,' the old woman said. 'I read doom in your palm long ago. You carry it inside yourself.'

Staring down at the river below Purity wondered how long it would take for the deed to be done. Useless to speculate for she would never know what had happened. The red-haired fellow would wait in vain for his money; Benjamin Rathbone would suspect — but she had no idea if his suspicions would hit anywhere near the truth. And when a little time had elapsed she would confide to Jessie that her husband had deserted her.

It was cold under the moon. She turned and went back into the house.

'Mistress, shall I lock up now? I was abed, but thought I heard voices and hoofbeats.'

Janet, a wrapper about her head and shoulders, stood sleepily in the kitchen.

'The master has been called away. I'll leave the door on the latch against his return.' She answered calmly, her hand steady on the bolt.

'Shall I wait up, mistress?'

'No need. I'll sit up myself for a while. Good-night, Janet.'

'Good-night, mistress.' Janet yawned and padded back across the dim kitchen.

James might very well come back. The Romanies might not have kept the bargain, or he might have outridden their knives, or even taken a different road. It was probable that he was safe, and in that case he would return one day.

She went into the parlour and, bending to the tray, lifted each glass of red wine in turn and drained it.

'If only you had been a man of surer instincts,' she said aloud, 'you would have known that all the drinks were harmless. You would have known it was only a cruel jest of my own, because I have not learned how to love.'

But she would learn. James would come back as he had come back before and find her gentle and forgiving.

The wine had made her slightly dizzy. It would never do for him to come back and find her in her cups!

Giggling, she sat back on her heels, watching the moon flaunt her ripe beauty in the windless sky. In a little while she would take out the golden cup and wrap it as a homecoming present for James.

Meanwhile she remained where she was, and failed to notice that her laughter had turned to weeping.

THE END

Other titles in the Linford Romance Library

SAVAGE PARADISE
Sheila Belshaw

For four years, Diana Hamilton had dreamed of returning to Luangwa Valley in Zambia. Now she was back — and, after a close encounter with a rhino — was receiving a lecture from a tall, khaki-clad man on the dangers of going into the bush alone!

PAST BETRAYALS
Giulia Gray

As soon as Jon realized that Julia had fallen in love with him, he broke off their relationship and returned to work in the Middle East. When Jon's best friend, Danny, proposed a marriage of friendship, Julia accepted. Then Jon returned and Julia discovered her love for him remained unchanged.

PRETTY MAIDS ALL IN A ROW
Rose Meadows

The six beautiful daughters of George III of England dreamt of handsome princes coming to claim them, but the King always found some excuse to reject proposals of marriage. This is the story of what befell the Princesses as they began to seek lovers at their father's court, leaving behind rumours of secret marriages and illegitimate children.

THE GOLDEN GIRL
Paula Lindsay

Sarah had everything — wealth, social background, great beauty and magnetic charm. Her heart was ruled by love and compassion for the less fortunate in life. Yet, when one man's happiness was at stake, she failed him — and herself.

A DREAM OF HER OWN
Barbara Best

A stranger gently kisses Sarah Danbury at her Betrothal Ball. Little does she realise that she is to meet this mysterious man again in very different circumstances.

HOSTAGE OF LOVE
Nara Lake

From the moment pretty Emma Tregear, the only child of a Van Diemen's Land magnate, met Philip Despard, she was desperately in love. Unfortunately, handsome Philip was a convict on parole.

THE ROAD TO BENDOUR
Joyce Eaglestone

Mary Mackenzie had lived a sheltered life on the family farm in Scotland. When she took a job in the city she was soon in a romantic maze from which only she could find the way out.